"I'm curious—" His dark blue eyes speared her

"Do you always find it necessary to tackle a man to get him horizontal?"

"Ohh! I didn't tackle you. I tripped and fell against you." At the skeptical lift of his brow, Kit's temper rose past boiling point. "And I was *not* out to get you horizontal, vertical or even diagonal. I wouldn't have you dipped in fourteen-carat gold!"

"A tantalizing thought—"

"And I'm *not* sleeping with my lab assistant!" That took care of his previous insinuation.

There was a crash of a file drawer, followed by the urgent clatter of a typewriter.

Stephen folded his arms across his chest, a grin spreading across his face. "The office is happy to have such nasty gossip cleared up."

"You—you—"

"You're sputtering." He took a step closer and pulled her against him, laughing softly. "Shut up, Kit." He leaned forward and kissed her.

Day Leclaire credits her husband and her family as being the prod that got her writing initially and kept her writing until she sold her first book to Harlequin. Although her young son consistently devises new and more ingenious methods to distract her from her computer (''I just wanted to see if the smoke detector really worked. Can you play with me now?'') her husband is equally clever at keeping Day slaving away (''I see McDonald's is hiring!'').

When she does take a break from writing, Day loves to go for a drive with her husband and son, especially along the coast near their San Diego home.

Jinxed
Day Leclaire

Harlequin Books

TORONTO • NEW YORK • LONDON
AMSTERDAM • PARIS • SYDNEY • HAMBURG
STOCKHOLM • ATHENS • TOKYO • MILAN

ISBN 0-373-03028-2

Harlequin Romance first edition January 1990

This book is dedicated to:

Merry Miss Sunshine
NANCY CECELIA TOTTON
A sister. A loving daughter.
A special friend
to all who knew and loved her.
We miss you.

CHAPTER ONE

"YOU *IDIOT*!"

A thick cloud of purple powder wafted out from under the laboratory door, spinning lazily in the artificially circulated air before settling gently on the pristine, cream-colored carpet. The door abruptly thumped open, emitting a huge puff of the brightly colored powder, along with two people coated from head to foot in the purple soot.

"You idiot!" the shorter of the pair repeated furiously, whipping off a pair of goggles, incongruously exposing two round circles of white skin. Snapping golden-brown eyes, sparking with ire, glared upward at her tall, thin male companion, and she threw down her goggles in disgust, choking on the resulting purple dust that mushroomed up from the carpet. "How could you have been so clumsy?" she sputtered once she was able to clear her clogged throat.

"I said I was sorry, Kit," the other shouted back. "What do you want, blood? It was an accident! I was thirsty and the water just spilled."

"Into both the ammonium nitrate and ammonium chloride?" Kit snapped, practically jumping up and down in her fury. "How is that possible, Todd? The compounds would have had to be already mixed with the zinc and iodine to get that sort of reaction."

Todd shoved a lock of once-black hair off his brow, leaving a brilliant purple streak across his forehead, and glared at her from his superior height. "That's gratitude for you! I was trying to do you a favor. Just trying to be helpful by having the chemicals premixed and all ready to go. But do you appreciate it? Oh, no, of course not.''

Kit's eyes squeezed shut for a brief moment, seeing again the dense, billowing cloud of purple smoke rising to swallow them when the water had come into contact with the chemicals. ''Why in the world did you have to make it in such a large quantity?'' The question was issued through gritted teeth and, as though knowing Todd wasn't about to give her an answer, she added, ''We only needed a tenth of what you prepared, if that.''

At Todd's silent shrug, Kit's wry, topaz eyes surveyed the filthy hallway and formerly cream carpet and then looked through the open door of the laboratory to see the violet powder slowly settling in a heavy blanket over the once spotlessly white interior. ''Damnation! What a mess. St. Clair is going to throw a fit if he gets wind of it. Just who do you think is going to clean up all this stuff?''

''Precisely what I was about to ask,'' a deep voice broke in. In unison, Todd and Kit turned toward the man who had unexpectedly appeared behind them, their mouths dropping open at the sight of him. ''I'm afraid St. Clair *has* just got wind of your little fiasco. Literally.''

Kit groaned, swearing silently and virulently beneath her breath. With undisguised dismay, she surveyed the tall, stern man standing before them, abject horror darkening her eyes.

A cold little smile played about his well-formed mouth, a smile that did not touch the startling blue of his wintry eyes. A smile that obviously did not indicate appreciation of the light dusting of violet that clung to his long gold lashes and to the burnished gold of his hair. And a smile that certainly did not care for the bright coating of powder that had settled into the deep creases of his rugged face. Nor did the damage stop there. Kit's wide golden-brown eyes gazed downward over his broad shoulders and muscular chest, all encased in an impeccably tailored tan suit—liberally dusted with purple powder.

"I was interested in the experiment, so I entered the lab through the other door." Long, muscular arms folded across a broad chest, the movement causing violet dust to waft serenely away from his large body. "And guess what happened?"

Why, she groaned inwardly, did this always happen to her? The moment something went awry, St. Clair was sure to be there, his slightly crooked nose flaring in disdain, his mouth curled mockingly, his frosty blue eyes reducing her to a quivering mass of jelly. "Mr. St. Clair, I'm really sorry," Kit finally said weakly. "We were trying to improve the magician's package and—"

"And I presume, Miss Mallory, you did your customary fine job and made a royal mess of things," he cut in curtly, his icy gaze sweeping over Kit as he shook his head in disbelief at her appearance. "As usual." A tiny jolt shot through Kit's body, the touch of his eyes creating an actual physical sensation as they moved over her. "You know, Miss Mallory, everyone has insisted, despite these—" he waved a long-fingered hand toward the lab "—these incidents, that you're really quite an asset to the company. I must admit I was somewhat skeptical before, but now I'm downright incredulous."

"Mr. St. Clair—if you'd just allow me to explain—"

"Certainly. You have ten minutes to be in my office with your explanation. I'll be quite interested to hear why you shouldn't be fired on the spot." With that, he turned and stalked toward the bank of elevators, little swirls of dark lilac dust spinning out behind him. There he turned back to survey the silent duo, a small cloud of regal purple settling around his feet. "I suggest, Mr. Templeton, that you start cleaning up this disaster. Immediately!"

"Phew!" sighed Todd the moment the elevator doors had closed behind their austere employer. "I can't believe this is for real!"

"Well, believe it," Kit snapped at him, still very shaken from her latest encounter with the great man himself. "I have precisely ten minutes in which to clean this powder off me and get up to the penthouse. I don't suppose you have any suggestions about what I can change into? I certainly can't track this stuff all through the building." She brushed ineffectively at her slacks and lab coat, sneezing repeatedly as powder once again filled the air.

"Would you cut that out!" Then realizing how upset she was, for their encounter with St. Clair had not exactly left him unfazed, either, Todd added a little more kindly. "You hit the showers first, Kit, and I'll lend you my spare set of coveralls. I have jeans and a T-shirt I can use in my car."

"You must be kidding. I'll look ludicrous!"

"You'd look a darn sight more ludicrous running around in your altogether," Todd retorted tartly, then grinned as a sudden thought occurred to him. "Although considering St. Clair's temper, that might not be a bad idea."

Not a bad idea—humph, Kit fumed silently, stepping under the small shower head in the tiny closet-size stall. St. Clair was a giant iceberg from one end of his large body to the other. From that superintellectual brain of his, to his hard, frozen heart, right down to his tippytoes, the man was pure ice. Why, she could probably dance naked on his desk and he wouldn't turn a hair, just tell her in that snooty tone of **his** to stop wasting his time and get back to work. If she still had a job, that was!

She twisted the knob of the faucet, howling her displeasure as freezing water cascaded onto her unprepared flesh. Naturally, she thought, her usually smiling mouth twisted into a snarl. What does an iceman need with hot water? It might actually thaw him out a bit. Ruthlessly, she thrust her head under the frigid water, pulling harshly at the braided strand of her normally honey-blond hair, watching as great pools of swirling purple gathered around her feet. Groping for the soap, she lathered her head, sighing her relief as the hot-water heater finally kicked in.

She paused momentarily, her hands sunk deeply in her sudsy scalp as the possibility struck her once again. Good grief! She could actually be fired! After only three months on the job, she could be back out on the streets searching for another position—and with the reference St. Clair was likely to give her, it would be a long search. She rinsed her hair, her hands moving automatically to wash her violet-streaked face as her brain raced along.

And all because she was a woman. Of course, nothing had actually been said. But she knew; she could tell. St. Clair's initial reaction when he had first met her had been a dead giveaway. How thunderous his expression had become, swiftly replaced by that cold, remote facade of his.

Kit's brow wrinkled in confusion. Why in the world had Miss Dobson, the personnel director, appointed a woman as head of The Toy Company's Testing and Research department when Stephen St. Clair so clearly preferred a man for the job? True, Miss Dobson was rather...umm, Kit smiled fondly. Well, Miss Dobson did tend to be a wee bit absentminded. Her smile turned to a grin. All right, if she was being perfectly honest, Miss Dobson was *very* absentminded. But even so, that didn't explain an obvious case of crossed wires between the president of the company and the head of personnel.

Kit's hands moved over her body, soaping away purple powder that had managed to find its way into the most interesting spots. And now, here she was, in the soup again for another minor disaster. How could it be that, in the space of a few short months, a reasonably intelligent mature woman of twenty-five could be instantly reduced to a klutz every single time a certain haughty, superior male came anywhere near her. Kit shook her head in annoyance, giving her sleek body a final rinse before turning off the steady spray of water.

Stepping out of the tiny cubicle, she grabbed a large, fluffy towel, thoughtfully provided by the company, and roughly began to rub the long strands of her hair. There wasn't time to dry it, but if she toweled most of the water out and rebraided it, it should pass muster.

"Are you going to be all day?" a man's voice bellowed. "You've got exactly two minutes and counting to be upstairs."

"Great!" she shouted back, briskly rubbing the remaining moisture from her tingling skin. "Should I go up wrapped in a damp towel? I thought you promised me something to wear."

"Got it right here, my lovely." She could hear the teasing leer in Todd's voice. "Should I bring it in?"

"Only if you want to have a cold shower—with your clothes on!"

His laughter echoed through the tiled dressing room. "I think I'll just leave it out here for you. Don't be too long—I think this purple stuff is beginning to give my skin a permanent tint."

Kit scooped up her discarded clothing, eyeing it with disfavor. Even her underclothes hadn't escaped contamination. She rinsed her lacy bra and bikini briefs in the sink, hoping the thin material would dry by the time her interview with St. Clair was completed.

In the dressing room she found the coveralls Todd had left for her, and her mouth curved upward in amusement. On Todd's six-foot-three-inch frame, the coverall, a one-piece outfit with long sleeves, fit very nicely. On her five-feet four-inches the result was going to be laughable, to say the least. Still . . . She cocked her head consideringly. The excessive amount of material, in a very masculine chocolate brown, should help conceal her lack of underclothes.

At least she hoped it would, feeling a twinge of concern as she pulled the zipper up the front of the coverall. Unfortunately it didn't extend all the way up, ending at least five inches too low on her chest, exposing a great deal of creamy skin from her throat down to the deep valley between her breasts—breasts that were noticeably unhindered by any kind of garment. Kit frowned, unpinning Todd's large name tag from the pocket of the coveralls and inserting the reassuringly heavy pin just above the thrust of her breasts. There, that should do it. She rolled up the dark brown sleeves and bent to do the same with the cuffs—it wouldn't do to trip and break her leg—acutely aware that her remaining minutes were rapidly ticking away. A final check to make sure her braid was neat and Kit hurried from the small dressing area.

A hesitant voice halted her headlong flight through the lobby. "Kathy? A moment, if you please."

Kit sighed and turned to face Miss Dobson, silently cursing the fates determined to keep her from reaching her employer's office within the stipulated ten minutes. "It's Kit, Miss Dobson, not Kathy," she corrected gently, a friendly smile coming to her lips at the sight of the sweet, diminutive lady who stood before her with the usual bundle of files tucked beneath her arm.

The head of personnel was quite elderly—not that her age had any noticeable effect on her abilities. Miss Dobson seemed to have an uncanny instinct for matching the right person with just the right job. She was regarded with fond amusement by most of the employees of The Toy Company, for she was famous for her absentmindedness and the peculiar way she seemed to pop in and out of places at the oddest moments. "What can I do for you, Miss Dobson?" Kit asked with an indulgent smile,

"They've moved Mr. Jenkins's office again!" Miss Dobson declared, practically dancing with righteous indignation. "How they expect a body to find their way when they keep moving everything about is beyond comprehension." Her twinkling blue eyes peered hopefully at Kit over wire-rimmed glasses perched on the end of what could only be called an inquisitive nose. "I don't suppose you know where they've put him this time, do you, my dear?" she asked with a tiny, wistful sigh.

Ruthlessly Kit forced back a laugh, not wanting to offend the rather vague woman, but at the same time knowing that Mr. Jenkins had occupied the same office for the past five years. Well, she was already late. What was another few minutes? "Of course, Miss Dobson," she said with a smile, adding kindly, "Why don't I take you there myself?"

"Thank you, my dear," Miss Dobson breathed in relief, peeking up at Kit as they headed down one of the gleaming white hallways. "And how are you settling down, Karen? Do you like our little company?" Miss Dobson questioned warmly, her tiny frame never still, as she flitted like a hummingbird alongside Kit. "We do want our employees to be happy here."

"Yes, Miss Dobson," Kit responded dutifully, and perfectly honestly. "I like it very much."

"No problems, dear?" Miss Dobson queried delicately, busily tucking a floating wisp of white hair behind one ear. "Sometimes when we try a little too hard, we find ourselves making a bit of a mess of things." Her bright blue eyes widened in distress behind the gleam of her lenses, her movements briefly stilled before resuming in a nervous frenzy of movement. "Not that you'd ever make a mess of things, my dear," she hastened to add, a tiny hand fluttering helplessly in the air. "But sometimes..."

Kit shut her eyes, suppressing a groan of exasperation. If the rather abstracted Miss Dobson was aware of the incident in the lab, then the whole office complex must be talking about it. "Everything's fine, Miss Dobson," Kit said, attempting to dismiss the subject with a measure of calm. "Honestly, it isn't anything I can't handle."

"Well, if you say so," Miss Dobson murmured doubtfully.

Kit's lips twitched with reluctant humor at the uncertainty in the older woman's voice, wondering wryly if her poor, abused ego was up to the battering still to come from St. Clair. "I say so," she stated firmly. "Mr. Jenkins's office is the next door on the left. Is there anything else I can help you with before I go?" she asked, knowing she was already unforgivably late, but unwilling to leave until she was certain Miss Dobson was taken care of.

"No, Miss Mallory, you've been a dear girl to put up with my bumbling ways."

Kit glanced down at Miss Dobson, some slight change in the older woman's voice capturing her attention. She was surprised to see a sudden sharpness in the older woman's eyes.

"Don't let Stephen bully you too much, Kit. You stand right up to him if he tries it." Miss Dobson's snowy head tilted thoughtfully to one side. "Of course, I wouldn't have hired you if I hadn't been certain you were the perfect one for him."

For a moment Kit was speechless. "You mean perfect for the job, don't you, Miss Dobson?" she finally managed to say.

Blue eyes twinkled brightly from behind the gleam of her spectacles. "Of course, dear. Isn't that what I said?" And with that she turned in the opposite direction from Mr. Jenkins's office and disappeared swiftly down the hallway, leaving an extremely bewildered Kit blinking in her wake.

You're late! You're late! The refrain echoed through Kit's brain as she rushed into St. Clair's outer office and looked around the silent room. No secretary, she noted with dismay. Now what? Her tawny eyes fell on the door leading to his private sanctum, noticing that it was slightly ajar, and without further thought she was across the room, shoving the door open and stepping into his office.

A small sound from the far side of the room drew her eyes and with a soft gasp, Kit realized her error in not first knocking. For there, through the open door of the en suite bathroom, stood her employer. He had his back to her and was completely naked, except for a thick, black towel slung casually around his lean, narrow hips, sluicing water over his golden head and wide, tanned shoulders in an attempt to rid himself of the brilliant violet powder that clung to his skin.

Kit sucked her breath in harshly, her eyes unnaturally large in her face, her heart pounding erratically, unable to tear her gaze from the enticing movement of well-developed muscles rippling across his back. Forcing her legs to move, Kit took a stumbling step backward. But it was too late.

"Is it your intention to stand there all day indulging your voyeuristic tendencies, or do you intend to pull your curious little nose out of my private office and knock like any civilized person would have?" a harsh voice blasted her in disgusted tones. Brilliant scarlet color flared into Kit's previously pale face as St. Clair whipped around to confront her, his hands on his hips.

"*Oh!*" She gulped, nearly falling over backward in her haste to get out the door. "Oh, my goodness, I'm sorry!" She hurriedly pulled the door shut with a bang, leaning her forehead against its cool surface in an agony of embarrassment. Why? Why? *Why?* It wasn't fair. It never failed that he brought out the worst in her. Just once she'd like to show him that she was good, really good, at her job, instead of the total screwup he thought her to be.

But, my God, he's beautiful, a small voice inside her head said in irreverent amazement. A hint of confusion darkened Kit's golden-brown eyes and, nibbling her lower lip, she wondered why the mere sight of a bare chest, on a man she considered cold and austere, was so distracting. How was it possible that this iceman—always careful to display such rigid perfection in his elegant three-piece suits and subdued ties—could have such a sensuous body, with that taut golden skin and that beguiling play of firm muscles just begging to be touched and caressed. And then, with a hint of a smile curling her mouth, Kit thought that he'd probably be shocked to the core of his frigid little heart if he could read her mind right now.

Of course, it had to be just then that he opened the door. And naturally, Kit fumed, she had to be caught grinning like an idiot and then fall like a ton of bricks against his broad, once again impeccably groomed chest. At least he was fully dressed, she thought dazedly, struggling to pull herself free of his arms. Finally she was able to stand upright and away from him on her own two, rather shaky, legs. She peeked nervously up at her employer and cringed inwardly at his stormy visage.

"What is it with you? Can't you do anything right?" Stephen St. Clair demanded, icy blasts chilling her from his narrowed eyes, glistening drops of water quivering in his still-damp hair. "Is it just me or are you like this with everyone you meet?"

"No, I'm not!" Kit retorted indignantly, squirming uncomfortably when it occurred to her that there could, just possibly, be a grain of truth in his words. "At least I don't think so," she added with painful honesty.

Stephen folded his arms across his chest, with, for the first time, a spark of amusement warming the frost in his eyes, turning them to a brilliant sapphire. "Then which is it? Or should I say *isn't* it—everyone or just me?"

Kit flipped her honey-blond braid backward over her shoulder and faced him with her hands on her hips. Unfortunately the effect wasn't quite what she might have wished, considering her small stature and the droopy fit of the oversize coveralls. "Let me assure you that I do not spend my life going from one disaster to another."

"That's a relief," Stephen murmured, enjoying the gold flash of ire that leaped into her large, tawny eyes.

Kit could feel her temper flaring and strove to control it. "For some reason, it's only when you are around that things inexplicably go wrong," she informed him tightly.

"I see, so now it's all my fault that you are hopelessly incompetent." Stephen shook his head, striding over to his desk and picking up a thick file. "I think that is open to debate," he said caustically, flipping through the folder.

"That's not what I—"

"Let me see. I believe I can find something in here to dispute that. Ah, yes." A lightning-blue glance speared her. "How about the Webber Films incident?" He fired the question at her, plucking several closely typed pages from the file and holding them up for her inspection.

Kit winced slightly. "The Mobley Monster worked fine in the lab. Some of the wires must have worked loose during shipping." She moved restlessly beneath his relentless gaze, thinking of the automated creature that was a cross between the Loch Ness monster and a giant slug with fangs. Webber Films had specially requested The Toy Company to dream up that particular creation for one of their science fiction adventure movies.

Stephen's eyes released her, dropping back down to the sheet in his hands. "It says here that the director was in the hospital for two weeks after your monster attacked him."

Kit's chin lifted a rebellious inch, a tinge of red creeping across her cheekbones. "Well, Webber Films couldn't have been that upset about it, considering they ordered a whole line of Tarantula Terrors for their next horror flick," Kit retorted with the merest hint of arrogance.

Stephen was swift to deflate her. "Mmm. I'm not sure you can say the same for the director. He's suing us." His attention returned to the file in his hand. "And then there was this small problem you had with—" he broke off, peering closely at a page "—a skateboard?" His eyebrows were raised inquiringly.

Kit shuffled her feet, chagrined, feeling like a schoolgirl called before the principal. "Todd and I were testing it out in the parking lot. No one was injured!"

"It says here that the sod replacement ran to the tune of—" he paused, flipping swiftly through the sheets of paper "—five hundred and thirty-nine dollars and fifteen cents."

Kit stalked up to the desk and snatched the receipt from his fingers. "I find that very hard to believe." Her eyes ran swiftly over the figures. "I thought not. One hundred and eighteen of it was for replacing the shrubs and forty-five was for new flowers. Besides, if Mrs. Enright hadn't panicked and driven up over that curb and onto the lawn—"

He returned the receipt to the file. "I see. Now it's Mrs. Enright's fault for trying to avoid running you down when you appeared out of nowhere directly in front of her car. On a skateboard."

"How else were we supposed to test it?" she challenged crossly. "We couldn't very well go whizzing through the halls."

His firm mouth twitched as the potential of that particular possibility leaped to his mind. "True, Miss Mallory. I'm quite relieved that the idea didn't occur to either you or Mr. Templeton."

Kit judiciously decided to ignore his last comment. She supposed he did have some cause to be a trifle peeved. But, after all, wasn't her department called Testing and Research? Just how did he expect her to do her job if she couldn't actively try out the product and make any necessary adjustments and improvements? "I notice you don't mention any of our successes. What about our series on warships? You certainly can't claim anything went wrong with that!" she threw at him triumphantly.

As Stephen flipped the file closed, the look he turned on her was ironic. "Very true. Even I would be amazed if you had found some way to turn the building of a simple model ship, designed for seven-year-olds, into a disaster area. The only thing you had to work with were the parts of the ship and the glue." His words stopped abruptly as he saw the pink color flooding her face. "Don't tell me," he murmured, shutting his eyes and shaking his head.

"Oh, why do you have to treat me like a two-year-old? Do you have any idea how that makes me feel?" she said resentfully, stomping away from him. "I only had to cut off three inches and I keep my hair in a braid now." She grabbed the long, blond plait and shook it at him.

He couldn't help it. His mouth began to twitch and then a deep, uninhibited laugh broke free, echoing around the room.

"Don't you laugh at me!" Kit snapped, thoroughly incensed. "Don't you dare!"

Stephen shook his head, moving away toward a small dressing area across the room. Kit followed right on his heels, endeavoring to keep from pummeling him from behind. "I can't believe you," he finally managed to choke out, picking up a gold tie clip from the top of a small dresser. "You're absolutely hopeless."

Kit fought to keep a tight rein on her volatile temper. "Mr. St. Clair, I realize this all looks very bad." She addressed the breadth of his back in a softer, more conciliatory tone, deciding that if she wanted to keep her job, she'd be much better off not antagonizing him. "But I promise you this will never happen again."

But, actually, it not only happened again, but no sooner were the words out of her mouth than the cuff at her ankle decided to come unrolled, tripping Kit and sending her careening full against her employer. She didn't weigh much, but he received the full impact of what there was of her and hit the floor like a felled tree, his nose unexpect-

edly buried in the two-inch-thick carpet, a horrified Kit
sprawled facedown across his back.

For a long moment Kit remained stunned and totally
immobile, her senses overwhelmed both by the enormity
of her position and by the unfamiliar feel of a hard male
body beneath her soft curves. But she didn't have long to
dwell on the strange sensations assailing her, for the deep
growl rumbling through Stephen's rigid body reminded her
of the precariousness of her situation.

"Are you some kind of walking disaster area?" His
muffled roar resounded around the room, his amusement
evaporating as his temper exploded like a volcano.

"I'm sorry!" Kit cried, galvanized into instant action.
She attempted to scramble backward off him, but found
she couldn't, the front of the coveralls unexpectedly preventing her.

Stephen St. Clair raised his face out of the carpet, vi-
ciously spitting loose fibers out of his mouth. "What the
hell are you doing? Get off me!"

"I'm sorry," she repeated feverishly, craning her neck
to peer down at the front of her coveralls. "I don't believe
it. This can't be happening to me," she moaned despairingly beneath her breath.

"Tell me very quickly and very precisely just what is
going on! Because if you're not off me in five seconds, I
swear I won't be responsible for my actions!"

Kit began to struggle in earnest, yanking at the pin that
had become firmly attached to the back of his shirt. "I'm
caught! I'm trying to get up, honestly I am, but I think the
name tag has somehow gotten caught in your shirt."

"Then undo it!" he thundered.

"If you'd just hold still, instead of bucking around like
a bronco, I could," she snarled back at him, her temper
finally cracking through her self-restraint. "I'm not a
complete imbecile."

"That is precisely what you are, Miss Mallory. An imbecile. I knew it the moment I laid eyes on you. It was perfectly apparent. So why I kept you on, I'll never know. Perhaps it's contagious and now I'm an imbecile as well."

"Stop twitching!" Kit ordered tightly, as his erratic squirming sent a riot of unexpected sensations racing through her. What in the world was wrong with her? With desperately fumbling fingers, Kit ripped at the stubborn pin. There was the faint, ominous sound of rending cloth and, like a shot, Kit rolled off Stephen's back and put a healthy distance between herself and the extremely irate male who was slowly rising to his feet. She inhaled raggedly, wondering why her body had chosen this particular moment to short-circuit, leaving her nerve endings crackling with a strange electrical charge.

For a moment Stephen said nothing, but instead twisted around in an attempt to peer over his shoulder before turning back to confront her. "I hope that sound I heard came from your elegant little getup and not from my brand-new silk shirt!" The words were forced out from between his stiff lips, his burning blue eyes searing her fearful gold ones.

Flinching ever so slightly, Kit slowly shook her head. "It was your shirt," she whispered. How she could ever have thought this blast furnace of a man to be made of ice, Kit didn't quite know. She shivered apprehensively. Stone, perhaps, but then, only if it was molten rock. "I—I'm sorry, Mr. St. Clair, it was an—"

In three swift steps he was across the room, his face thrust toward hers until they were practically touching. "You, Miss Mallory, are not only an imbecile, but a jinx!" His warm breath blew across her face like an arid desert wind. "You should have a ten-foot no-man's-land around you, and even then you'd *still* be a walking disaster area!"

"And you, Mr. St. Clair, are a misogynist," Kit retorted sweetly, unexpectedly hurt by his harsh words.

Then, thrusting her daintily upturned nose disdainfully toward his slightly crooked one, she insisted fiercely, "If you would just listen to me—"

"All I seem to do *is* listen to you. One excuse after another, after another. Well, lady, you've just run out of excuses."

Kit's teeth snapped together, fury swamping every other thought and consideration. Any idea of attempting to placate the man was shoved firmly to one side. "How dare you! You've had it in for me every since I started working here. Do you think I haven't heard the rumors?"

She saw the muscles in his face tighten, and knew that the tiny lines crinkling around his eyes were not due to amusement. But she no longer cared. "And what rumors were those, Miss Mallory?" he asked softly.

Anger made Kit incautious, sweeping away any remaining thought of following Miss Dobson's advice. "That you are prejudiced against women, that's what. And personally, I find that all too easy to believe."

"Do you now?" She never heard the warning in his voice, intent only on finally telling him what she really thought of him.

"Yes!" Her eyes sparkled with defiance. "Yes," she repeated in a less vehement tone, but with equal determination. "It's apparent that you're nothing but a prejudiced, old-fashioned, male chauv—"

Abruptly she broke off, stepping back a pace, her tawny eyes blinking in sudden alarm at the small threatening sound coming from between his clenched teeth, a sound that silenced her more effectively than anything else could have. "Don't say it," he bit out furiously. "Don't you dare use that hackneyed, overused, abusive phrase with me!"

Wide-eyed, Kit stared into the forbidding countenance before her, seeing the rage he fought to suppress. Rage directed solely at her. "You know nothing about me. Nothing! My feelings and attitudes toward women are personal and, therefore, none of your business. So you keep your petty little judgments and nasty gossip about my private life to yourself. Have you got that, Miss Mallory?'' Slowly Kit nodded her head, realizing that she'd pushed him too far.

Abruptly he moved away from her, the taut muscles of his shoulders shifting restlessly beneath the fine silk of his shirt. Several tense minutes ticked by before he turned back to face her. Forcing a calmer tone into his voice, Stephen continued. ''If, on the other hand, you wish to discuss your so-called employment with this company and my attitude toward you as an employee, believe me, it will be my pleasure. Why don't we begin with how you managed to con poor Miss Dobson into giving you a job you're obviously incapable of performing!'' The words were flung down like a gauntlet.

''Con!'' Kit gasped.

''Yes, Miss Mallory, the word I used was con. Explain how, when I specifically requested a man for the position you now hold, you managed to get the job.''

Kit started to protest, but his voice overrode her, obviously unwilling to allow her an opportunity to comment. ''Miss Dobson assured me that she'd hired a man for your job and then, not two days later, I was introduced to you!''

His blue eyes began to flash, irritation bringing a renewed anger to his words. ''And after the series of catastrophes you've engineered, you have the unmitigated gall to question my dissatisfaction with your performance? I find that incredible to say the least, considering you have single-handedly managed to turn this company upside down, from a smoothly run, top-notch corporation, to the laughingstock of the industry. And all in the space of a mere three months!'' His voice rose to a bellow.

It was too much. She couldn't—no, wouldn't—listen to another minute of his abuse and half-truths. She was as good as fired anyway, so what more could he do to her? With a voice quivering with indignation, Kit said evenly "I believe what you attempted, Mr. St. Clair, is called sexual discrimination. And unless the law has been changed in the last three months, you could find yourself on the wrong end of a very nasty suit."

"Are you threatening me, Miss Mallory?" Stephen's golden eyebrows shot skyward incredulously. "Considering the fact that you presently hold the position in question, you might find that claim a trifle difficult to prove. And if I fired you this minute, I can guarantee you that there isn't a court in the land that would consider that I've discriminated against you—certainly not once they've examined the list of your dubious accomplishments!"

Kit shook her head, forcing herself not to reveal her consternation. "I'm not threatening you," she retorted with quiet dignity. "I'm merely attempting to defend myself against some rather unfair charges. I was hired on the sole basis of my qualifications—and if you check my personnel file, you'll find they're excellent. As for Miss Dobson's assurances that she'd hired a man, I can guarantee you that it would be a little difficult to conceal the fact that I'm a female, even if that had been my intention. She obviously considered that job performance was more important to you than your employee's sex. Miss Dobson may be a trifle vague about some things, Mr. St. Clair, but I can assure you that she isn't so unobservant as to mistake the fact that I'm a woman!"

For a moment there was dead silence in the room and Kit was aware that her fate balanced on the edge of a very sharp sword. She could tell that he was listening seriously to her impassioned declaration, and was weighing her words with care. She waited, knowing that she would serve herself best by remaining silent and letting him work it out in his own mind. And then a rakish grin spread over Stephen St. Clair's face, taking Kit completely by surprise.

"Well," he drawled, his eyes skimming over her. "You've got me there. I don't suppose anyone could describe that figure as boyish."

Kit felt sudden heat flood her body. Her curves had always been quite generous, but until this moment she had never before felt self-conscious about it. Nor had she ever felt such an intense recognition of her own femininity. She could actually feel the fiery touch of his eyes on the fullness of her breasts, his gaze lighting a small fire as it passed down over the sharp indent of her waist and on to the shapely flare of her hips and thighs.

Kit's breath quickened at her physical reaction to him, praying that he wouldn't sense it. She was horrified by the response she was feeling and equally horrified at her inability to repress her unexpected awareness of him as a man. And this wasn't just any man—this was her employer!

Stephen's intense, blue gaze narrowed on the molten-gold blaze that leaped into her eyes, misinterpreting what he read there. "And before you start accusing me of sexual harrassment—"

Kit took a stumbling step backward. "I'm not! I wasn't! Just—just stop looking at me like that!" Kit couldn't prevent the defensive retort from spilling from her lips, realizing instantly that she had said and done exactly the wrong thing. She could see the sudden understanding dawn in his expression as the smile on his face spread into a broad grin.

"What's the matter?" he asked with a gentleness that made her suddenly very nervous. "Have I frightened you? Are you afraid that the iceman is going to lose control of his nonexistent emotions?" At her strangled gasp he inclined his golden head. "You thought I didn't know that you called me that, did you? I knew. And now you're worried about what? That I'm about to go berserk, drag you to the floor and have my wicked way with you? How positively Victorian, Miss Mallory,'' Stephen drawled.

He stepped toward her, his sapphire eyes capturing hers with a look that took her breath away. Not daring to so much as blink, Kit waited for him to make the next move.

But the next move came from an entirely different source. The sound of the door opening made them both jump and Kit's dazed eyes turned toward the elegant woman who stepped through the doorway, a woman whose cold, brown eyes took the situation in with one swift glance, and then hardened perceptively. ''My, my,'' she remarked, her deep husky voice laced with amusement and a hint of distaste. ''Not reduced to chasing after the hirelings, are we, Stephen, dearest? What would people say?''

CHAPTER TWO

"Yes, hello."

"Hello, Kitten. How are you doing?"

"Hi, Mom." Kit dropped onto the couch, stretching her feet out to rest on the marble-topped coffee table in front of her and yawned widely. "I'm fine. How about yourself?"

She could hear her mother's light laughter drifting across the phone wires and smiled tiredly in response. "A lot better than you, by the sound of things. Still working such long hours?"

Kit shrugged, aware of her mother's sympathy and relaxing beneath its comforting balm. "Not really. I mean, they keep me busy, but I like being busy. Actually I prefer it. And any overtime hours I put in are because I choose to."

"Well, I worry about you, darling. You know I do. I just hope that job doesn't prove to be too much for you."

Kit chuckled, teasing lightly, "But, Mom, weren't you the one who insisted that playing with toys all day couldn't possibly be considered real work?"

"Did I say that?" Kit could hear the laughing chagrin in her mother's voice. "I'm sure that wasn't me. It must have been that other mother—the one who's always nagging you."

"Right. I remember her. She's the one who likes to say things like 'once a mother, always a mother.'"

Elizabeth Mallory's warm laughter came clearly over the line as she joined in a game that had begun when Kit was a teenager. "And I'm sure I've heard her ask lately when you were planning on finally settling down with a husband, a house and 2.4 children."

Kit winced, having heard that particular comment more than once. "Well, I hope you put the woman firmly in her place."

Kit's mother was quick to reassure her. "Oh, I did, I informed her in no uncertain terms that my daughter had absolutely no intention of tying herself down to any mere man. Her career comes first, I said."

"How brave of you!" Kit marveled. "What did our dear, pseudomother say to that?"

"Well—" Elizabeth Mallory paused dramatically before dropping her voice to a whisper "—don't tell her I told you this, but she suggested I invite you home for next weekend. Of course, the fact that Anne's brother Jesse will be here that same weekend hasn't a thing to do with it."

"Of course not!" Kit struggled to keep from laughing, knowing all too well her mother's romantic scheming. "I'll tell you, though, when I finally get to meet this person who's been impersonating you for the past ten years, I'm going to have a thing or two to say to her."

"If she lets you," came the dry retort. "Seriously, though, do you think you could make it next weekend? Your brother and sister-in-law were complaining that they haven't seen you in months."

"Well, you can tell Fredrik and Anne that I'll be there with bells on. I just hope you're not going to be too disappointed when I don't fall on Jesse like a starving man on a feast. As much as I like him, there just isn't that special spark between us."

Kit thought of Anne's brother, almost wishing she could drum up a warmer response to him. She knew her family would be ecstatic—and just possibly stop their incessant matchmaking. Unfortunately there wasn't anything there. No chemistry, no wild, tingly feeling way down deep as there had been—Kit bolted upright. Good grief, no! How in the world had Stephen St. Clair strayed into her thoughts like that?

True, on the surface he and Jesse shared the same good looks. Both were blond, blue-eyed and tall. But where Jesse had a very open, boyish sort of personality, Stephen's was much more complex. On the surface, her employer seemed coolly remote, but beneath that icy facade she'd discovered the fierce, explosive temper he'd been keeping in such firm check. It amazed her that she could have been so mistaken in her analysis of his character.

And physically there was no comparison, either. On the few dates they'd had Jesse had kissed her without stirring the least response. Yet with Stephen, just those brief minutes of contact when she'd been pinned to his back had aroused such a storm of reaction that she was still confused by it.

"Anne understands that you and Jesse are just friends, Kit." Her mother's voice was a welcome intrusion into her wayward thoughts. There was a brief moment's hesitation before Elizabeth Mallory continued. "She just wants to see you as happy as she and Fredrik are. I guess she feels that ever since Jeffery—"

"Ever since Jeffery, I've been more interested in my career," Kit cut in lightly. "Or so it seems to my very concerned and caring relatives. Mom, that was a long time ago. And though it hurt then, it doesn't now. I'm not single because of what happened with Jeffery. I just haven't met anyone I care for. At least not enough to make a lasting commitment."

"Or perhaps you haven't given anyone the chance to mean more to you than your job," her mother suggested quietly. "I'm sorry, darling, I didn't call up to preach. We just haven't seen you for a while and were hoping you'd come up.''

"No problem, I'll be there," Kit reassured her mother in a deliberately casual voice. But inwardly she felt her muscles tensing.

"Take care, Kitten. I love you.''

"Me, too, Mom." And with that the line went dead.

Fretfully Kit stood and paced the comfortable living area of the duplex she rented. She'd been expecting a call from her parents. After all, she'd been making any number of excuses to avoid visiting them for the past two months, so it was only a matter of time before they began to wonder. If only she didn't feel so uncomfortable about the whole situation. If only she could just tell them, straight out, what the problem was. It seemed, with a gradually increasing frequency, that each time she came to visit, either they, or Fredrik and Anne, had found someone new for her to meet. Not that she minded making new friends. But the continuous parade of eligible males trotted out for her inspection was beginning to be a grind.

Lately she'd gotten a series of mental images of the four of them sitting around the table, discussing her "predicament." Poor Kit, they'd say, shaking their heads grimly, twenty-five and still single. We've got to do something for her and things are beginning to get desperate. Can't you think of *someone* she hasn't met yet? She doesn't have a lot of good years left in her, you know.

A reluctant grin split her face as the crazy image faded. She felt so distanced from them at times. Even Anne, who had been her best friend all through high school and into college had more in common with her parents than she had. Her smile fell away, a hint of bewilderment touching her brow. All those years she and Anne had shared, all the dreams and goals—they'd all slowly dissipated over time. At least Anne's had. The career her friend had planned as an interior designer had been easily forgotten the moment Kit's brother, Fredrik, had appeared on the scene.

After meeting as children, the two hadn't seen each other for at least five years, with Fredrik relocating to the East Coast temporarily and Anne still a schoolgirl at the time he had left. But when, on a visit home with Kit, the two had been reintroduced, it had spelled the end of all Anne's ambitions save one: to marry Fredrik and produce their first son exactly nine months after their wedding, and their second son one year after that.

Not that there was anything wrong with marriage or babies. But the changes they wrought weren't something she particularly cared to experience. Kit wandered into her bedroom, pulling open the closet door and extracting the windbreaker hanging there. She needed some fresh air. She needed to think.

At the door, Kit slipped on a pair of sandals and went out, turning west toward the ocean. One of the main reasons she had decided to rent this particular duplex was its vicinity to the beach. Located in the beautiful resortlike village of Carlsbad on the coast of California, about thirty miles north of San Diego, the duplex was within a few scant miles of her job and a mere five blocks from the Pacific Ocean. And that was where Kit was headed. To the peace and serenity she found walking along the beach, with the cool saltwater lapping at her ankles and the grainy sand grating against the soles of her feet. It never failed to soothe her when things got to be too much. And today had been too much!

Her thoughts turned back to Anne. She knew a lot of women chose to give up their careers and become full-time housewives—if they could afford it. But the changes in her friend, someone Kit had thought she knew as intimately as herself, had confused and puzzled her. It had been the gradual distancing between them, though, that had proved to be the most painful wrench.

Kit crossed over the main street, Carlsbad Boulevard, completely oblivious of the drivers who slammed on their brakes and hit their horns as she stepped out directly into their path, totally engrossed in her thoughts. Walking south along the narrow, grassy strip that separated the old highway from the water, Kit gazed down from the small parklike area, high above the ocean, to the beach far below, a beach only recently made accessible at this point by newly cemented steps.

She and Anne used to joke about their comfortable middle-class parents, with their comfortable middle-class lives—lives filled with golfing and bridge clubs, PTA meetings and the occasional weekend trips to the desert or Las Vegas. Only it wasn't a joke anymore. Once Anne had shuddered at the prospect of leading a similar life to their parents', but now she practically reveled in it.

Kit sighed, staring outward across the ocean at the small sailboats that dotted the horizon, and at the surfers farther in where the waves were breaking, some of them in partial wet suits to insulate their bodies against the prolonged exposure to the chilly water. Finally her gaze shifted to the shoreline where the waves washed up onto the beach.

Even though it was mid-July, and quite warm during the day, a light misty cloud was rolling in, obscuring the slowly sinking sun, a brisk wind giving a slight chill to the usually temperate air. Kit pulled the hood of the windbreaker up over her head, turning to continue walking briskly along the sidewalk to the bridge that spanned the narrow channel between the ocean and Agua Hedionda Lagoon.

Kit wrinkled her straight little nose as she stepped onto the newly renovated bridge. A sulfur spring had inspired the lagoon's rather unfortunate name, which was Spanish for "stinking water." Now, however, the lagoon, which extended inland for about ten miles, was used for waterskiing and swimming, a small marina having been built toward the east end for that purpose.

She smiled at the fishermen who lined the pedestrian walkway, unaware that their eyes continued to follow her the full length of the bridge and even farther, to where she turned westward onto the state beach. There Kit stopped to remove her sandals and roll up the cuffs of her jeans before heading across the broad expanse of sand to the waterline.

A gusty breeze blew against Kit's face, lifting the hood of her jacket up and away from her head, teasing her honey-blond hair into attractive disarray. She gazed down the beach toward the flashing tower of San Diego Gas and Electric's Encina power plant and wondered if she had the energy to walk that far. Probably not. She sighed.

Once, about six months after Anne's marriage to Fredrik, she'd gotten up the nerve to ask Anne about her complete change in attitude. How could she, in the space of a few short months, go from the career-oriented, free-spirited woman she had been to—Kit couldn't conceal her shudder—a housewife?

"You'll see." Anne had laughed gently, not in the least offended by Kit's obvious distaste for her life-style. Her lovely blue eyes glowed warmly. "How can what I have compare with a career?" She'd shaken her head decisively, a protective hand curling about her distended stomach.

"But—" Kit had begun.

"You don't understand, Kit, because you've never been in love. One day you'll meet a man you can't live without. Someone you'd sacrifice anything and everything to be with. Then come and tell me how a career stacks up against that." There had even been the slightest hint of pity in her serene expression and Kit squirmed remembering it, for the first time feeling as though she'd missed out on something vital.

Gradually the feeling of exclusion had intensified until their former closeness had completely disappeared, leav-

ing Kit bewildered and slightly hurt by it all. But the hurt
hadn't lasted. There was too much going on in Kit's life for
her to brood about it for long—being out on her own in
her first apartment, new friends, the excitement of starting out in her chosen career—had all taken up her time and
energy. And though they were no longer on intimate terms,
she and Anne were still friendly.

Kit wrapped her arms around herself, pushing the sand
into small hills with her toes, frowning pensively. Looking back, she had no problem seeing and understanding the
divergent courses their lives had taken. It was only natural that marriage would change the focus of Anne's life,
causing her to give precedence to Fredrik and their children. But what she didn't understand was why her parents
were trying to push her into a similar mold.

And, despite what they obviously thought, her reluctance to go along with their hopes for her wasn't because
of Jeffery! She had emerged from that disaster relatively
unscathed. Sure, it had hurt—what love affair gone awry
didn't? But she wasn't foolish enough, or naive enough, to
assume that every man was going to be another Jeffery. Or
that there couldn't one day be someone capable of giving
her everything Jeffery had not. She just wasn't actively
looking for it, that was all. And she was damned if she'd
be pushed into a relationship because her well-meaning
and loving parents thought it best for her.

Was she overreacting? Kit wondered. To be perfectly
fair, she supposed it was possible that what she saw as her
parents' obsession to see her married was no more than
their desire for her happiness. What they didn't seem willing to recognize was that she *was* happy. Surely there
wasn't anything wrong with concentrating on a career?
When she fell in love—if she fell in love—would be the
proper time to worry about any conflicts between marriage and her job. And these days it was fairly rare to find
a wife who didn't work, if only out of pure necessity!

Well, if the mysteries of love and marriage were a trifle beyond her, the necessity of keeping her job was not. If she still *had* a job! Especially when she remembered what had happened after that hideous woman had entered Stephen's office.

"Not reduced to chasing after the hirelings, are we, Stephen, dearest? What would people say?" Kit could hear the stinging words all over again and she shivered.

The word that had issued softly from Stephen's lips was unexpectedly coarse, and with a disapproving frown, the woman had stepped farther into the room, closing the door sharply behind her.

"I've told you before not to use that kind of language around me!" the older woman fired at him, striding unhesitatingly to Stephen's desk and seating herself behind it in the large leather chair. She swiveled around to face them, those fierce, dark eyes taking in every minute detail of Kit's appearance, then fixing on the almost protective stance Stephen had assumed in front of her. The woman's mouth tightened.

"Stop cowering behind him like that," she snapped at Kit. "**I'm** not likely to harm you—a least not yet." For one moment longer the woman preserved her remotely harsh facade, and then it dropped from her, completely discarded in the face of her total exasperation. "Good grief, Stephen, what *are* you thinking about? Have you lost all sense of common decency? What if I'd been your secretary, or Lydia, for heaven's sake?"

Stephen had remained totally unmoved by the woman's diatribe, his arms folded impassively across his chest, the lines of his face taut in response to her disapproval. "Lydia would have had the courtesy to knock, Mother. And my secretary wouldn't have dared to enter without being told to do so first." Kit started. This horrible medusa was his *mother*? She nerved herself to peek around Stephen's shoulder and hastily drew back with a shudder. And she had thought Stephen was formidable. This woman would have made Lucrezia Borgia cower!

"I did knock!" the woman bit out, her deep voice radiating her ire. "But you were obviously so occupied with this—this—"

"Enough!" Stephen's low, harsh command brooked no debate. "You know nothing of the circumstances so I'll hear nothing further from you about it."

He looked down at Kit, pushing her reluctantly into the chair in front of his desk. "I'm afraid you'll have to stay here while I find myself another shirt. We still have a number of things to clear up." He turned a searing gaze on the forbidding woman behind his desk. "I have an extremely important meeting with a prospective client in precisely fifteen minutes. So please be brief when I return or, better yet, be gone."

"How kind you are!" his mother flashed back. "Believe me, I won't take up any more of your valuable time than absolutely necessary." She glanced quickly at Kit, then back at Stephen, clearly uncomfortable having to explain herself in front of the younger woman. "I—I'd like your advice on a personal matter, if you don't mind."

Stephen snorted unkindly. "That's a first. Very well, Mother. I'll just be a minute." He started across the room and then turned to face them, his eyes narrowing, a clear warning glistening in their ice-blue depths. "And do keep your sharp claws off this little morsel, Mother dear," he ordered softly, nodding toward Kit. "She's not in your league."

Kit watched him stride across the room to a door on the other side of the office and disappear through it. The woman actually waited a full sixty seconds before starting in on her. "It leads to his apartment." She inclined her head toward the door Stephen had just used. "His private little sanctum. Or did you know that already?"

"No, I did not!"

"Mmm." Her tone was disbelieving. Then she shrugged her wide shoulders in dismissal, fixing Kit with a cold, disparaging gaze. "Well, in case you hadn't figured it out," she began, in a tone implying that it was extremely unlikely that Kit could figure anything out, even something so very elementary as her identity, "I'm Victoria St. Clair, Stephen's mother." She leaned back in the chair, tossing her leather purse onto the desk, and crossed her shapely legs. "You—" the tone dripped icicles "—may call me Mrs. St. Clair."

Kit's delicate features tightened. Well! So much for sheathing her claws—this woman was out for blood. And Kit just might be willing to oblige her. Well, maybe. "And you may call me Miss Mallory," Kit retorted nicely, trying not to reveal her nervousness before those burning umber eyes.

If only the woman hadn't been so intimidating. But Kit was darned if she could detect a single flaw in Victoria St. Clair's sophisticated appearance. Even her height was overwhelming—at a guess she probably stood a full head above Kit.

Elegantly slender, she was dressed in a very expensive business suit, that was undoubtedly worth more than Kit's wages for a full month—maybe two. The worsted material's deep red color made a striking complement to the rich auburn of the older woman's glossy hair, which was pulled back into an elegant chignon, emphasizing her stunning bone structure. Nothing but the best for this woman, from the two-hundred-dollar-an-ounce perfume Kit detected, right down to the handmade two-hundred-dollar shoes that graced her feet.

Even her age was something of a mystery. The beautiful face across from her seemed untouched by time and Kit was certain that her makeup had been applied with an expert hand. Strong, winged brows arched over her brilliant, sharply intelligent eyes and a soft shade of ruby tinted her high cheekbones and full, stern mouth. She looked nothing like Stephen and yet, strangely, everything like Stephen.

Returning stare for stare, Victoria St. Clair reached for her purse, ruby-tipped nails snapping open the catch and extracting a thin, gold cigarette case and matching lighter. Calmly, her eyes never leaving Kit's, she selected a long, brown cheroot and put it between her glossy red lips. With a practiced movement, she flipped open the lighter and spun the tiny wheel, striking a small flame. Gracefully she bent her head toward the flame, touching it to the tip of her cheroot, then inhaled deeply.

Without warning, sharp brown eyes speared Kit like a bug on a pin and a slow smiled curled her mouth. "Fair warning, my girl. Don't try sparring with me," she instructed softly. "I'm as tough as they come and you'll get hurt if you go against me. Badly, if I have anything to say about it." She blew a long stream of smoke into the air. "Now tell me what you're doing in my son's office— practically embracing him, I might add," she ordered harshly.

For one insane moment, Kit thought she was going to dissolve onto the chair in a lump of soft, quivering gelatin. Lemon gelatin to be precise—a nice cowardly color. It came as a distinct shock when from out of nowhere she heard herself answer in a strong, firm voice. "No." Kit blinked once in pleased surprise and then managed a cool little smile to accompany her defiance.

That she had shocked Victoria St. Clair as much as she had herself was immediately apparent. Unable to find an ashtray, the woman placed her cheroot on top of a small dish of paper clips and leaned across the expanse of the desk, fixing her magnificent eyes in disbelief on Kit's stubborn face. "I beg your pardon? What did you say to me?"

"And so you should—beg my pardon." Suddenly Kit
was fed up. So far today she'd been practically smothered
in purple powder—courtesy of Todd—ridiculed, insulted,
disbelieved, and just short of manhandled—courtesy of
Stephen St. Clair—and now—courtesy of this hideous
woman—forced to tolerate her unbelievable insolence
without any protection from her son. Where on earth was
he hiding, anyway?

And to top it all off, she had had to endure the latter's
insults clothed in Todd's oversize coveralls. It was lowering, to say the least, in the face of Victoria St. Clair's perfection! With great deliberation, Kit crossed one leg over
the other, the cuff of her pants, unrolling to dangle child-
ishly off the end of her foot. Struggling desperately to keep
her expression from revealing her mortification, she retorted sweetly, "I thought I was perfectly clear. What word
didn't you understand?" She watched the fury erupt in
Victoria St. Clair's face before adding nonchalantly, "And
by the way, your cigarette has just set that paper on fire."

With a gasp, Victoria St. Clair was on her feet. Instead
of simply smothering the flames, she snatched up the
burning paper and dropped it hastily into the wastepaper
basket, jumping back in horror when great tongues of
flame shot up from the round aluminum can.

For a brief instant Kit sat with her mouth hanging open
in amazement. Then, realizing that the flames were rapidly getting out of control, Kit was at the door, yanking it
open. Just outside Stephen's office was a large red case
with protective glass covering it and a small hammer dan-
gling on a string. Not pausing for an instant, Kit snatched
up the hammer, smashed it against the glass, and attempted to grab the large fire extinguisher she found inside. She hadn't counted on its weighing so much, and
precious seconds disappeared while she struggled to pull it
from the case.

The moment the glass shattered, alarm bells started to ring shrilly throughout the office building and Kit, hearing Victoria St. Clair's voice shouting for her, finally managed to free the extinguisher, staggering back to Stephen's office and over to the flaming wastepaper basket. Heaving the heavy cylinder up into her arms, she aimed the nozzle and squeezed the trigger. A huge stream of foam burst from the extinguisher, the force of the blast tipping her over backward, and foam shot upward from her chest like an erupting volcano.

"Stop it! Turn it off!" she heard Victoria St. Clair shriek over the sound of the alarm.

The woman's screams finally penetrated. Kit pried her panic-frozen fingers from around the trigger of the fire extinguisher, and the foaming white volcano came to an abrupt halt. Several long seconds ticked by before Kit got up the nerve to look around her. Briefly a small cloud of smoke obscured Kit's view of the woman. Then the overhead sprinklers sputtered to life and the cloud cleared, revealing Stephen's mother covered from head to foot in white foam, foam that also covered every available surface in the room. Foam that was slowly sliding off a bedraggled Victoria St. Clair as water poured down from the ceiling, soaking her, Kit, and every single inch of Stephen St. Clair's office.

"WHY THE HELL was I worried about my mother tearing you to shreds? I should have been worried about what the hell *you'd* do to my mother!"

Kit cringed beneath the blast of fury that was directed her way. "But it wasn't my—"

"Oh, my God!" Stephen interrupted her, stopping his frenetic pacing in front of the large expanse of windows that lined one wall of his office.

He turned, scrambling for the phone, cursing at the splattering of water that poured into his ear from the wet receiver. "Milly, I thought I told you to call the fire department and explain things." He paused for an instant before blasting into the phone, "Well, it doesn't seem to have done any good, because every fire engine in Oceanside, Vista and Carlsbad is parked directly beneath this window... Well, now there's a brilliant suggestion! Why don't you just do that? And while you're at it, tell them to put away those damned hatchets they're so busy swinging around!" He slammed down the phone, glaring at Kit, his face turning from red to white to red again.

"I knew it—the second I heard those alarms go off. It had to be you. It just had to be. There wasn't anyone else it could have been!" He broke off, inhaling deeply, running a hand through his wet hair, standing the damp strands up on end. Then he exploded again. "Who the hell are you? Some sort of horrible secret weapon my competition discovered and planted on me?"

"You must be joking," Kit glared at him. "That's the most ridiculous thing I've ever heard."

"Ridiculous!" he shouted at her through clenched teeth. "I'm being ridiculous? Tell me, Miss Mallory, how did they do it? Did they program you, push a button and say 'Go. Seek. Destroy'? And off you went to ruin my life."

"Don't be absurd!" Kit snapped, not knowing whether to hit him or burst into tears, only knowing that he was hurting her, and that the pain she felt confused her. Why did it matter so much what Stephen St. Clair thought of her?

He advanced around the desk toward her, water bubbling up around his shoes, making funny little sucking sounds. "I'm not being ridiculous or absurd or even minutely nonsensical. I'm finally seeing clearly for the first time in three whole months. You're out to get me. That was your plan from the beginning—to drive me straight around the bend."

Kit caught sight of the wild light in his blazing blue eyes, and backed away from him in alarm, stumbling and sliding, until with a cry she tripped, and landed painfully on her backside, water squirting out on either side of her when she hit the drenched carpet.

"Stephen!" In unison Stephen and Kit turned toward the door that led to his private living area. Victoria St. Clair stood framed in the doorway, her deep voice commanding immediate attention.

Kit's eyes widened in amazement at the change in her. She'd taken the time to shower and was dressed in a floor-length bathrobe in a soft shade of rose. If it hadn't been for that distinctive, husky voice, Kit never would have believed it was the same person. Without any makeup and with her russet hair swirling around her shoulders she looked like—well, certainly like an entirely different person from the hard-hearted businesswoman of earlier. "Help the girl up."

Kit started in amazement. Her ears must be playing tricks on her. This could not be the same horrible woman. Why, she was actually being kind!

"Why the hell should I? In fact I can't think of a safer place to keep her!"

"Stephen, it wasn't her fault."

"It never is!"

"Oh, for heaven's sake, ease up." She crossed the room on bare feet, grimacing at the water that squelched up between her toes. "It was my cigarette that started the blaze. I'll admit Miss Mallory was a trifle overzealous in putting out the fire, but it was better than burning down the entire building." Now that sounded a little more true to form, Kit thought with a scowl, shoving a wet strand of hair out of her face.

"If you say so. I'm not so sure," he snapped, his glittering blue eyes glued to Kit's wilting figure. He reached down and hauled her to her feet, the woebegone expression on her exhausted face disturbing him far more than he cared to admit. Kit sneezed. "Don't you have some clothes you can change into?" he barked gruffly.

"Oh, sure," Kit muttered caustically. "I keep a whole wardrobe downstairs so that when your office is set on fire and the sprinklers go off, I'll have just the right outfit to change into."

Stephen glared down at Kit, seriously tempted to wring her neck. "Considering the number of accidents you seem to create, maybe you should think about it!"

Victoria St. Clair interrupted their renewed battle in a dry tone, waving a negligent hand at Kit's soggy coveralls. "Well, obviously she didn't. Otherwise she wouldn't be sporting her present costume. From an earlier incident, perhaps, Miss Mallory?" she inquired, her voice laced with amusement. When Kit remained stubbornly silent, Victoria shrugged, holding out a plain brown bag. "Here. I brought this down for you to change into."

Kit blinked in surprise, barely able to credit the hint of sympathetic understanding she read in Victoria St. Clair's dark brown eyes. "Thank you," she stammered, glancing uneasily at the strange expression on Stephen's tightly set features. "If I could just use your bathroom..." she murmured in a subdued voice, edging away from him, wondering nervously what he was thinking. She sneezed again.

Stephen rolled his eyes heavenward before waving an impatient hand toward the bathroom. "Feel free, Miss Mallory. Please. My home is yours. What's left of it, that is."

Kit bit her lip at his sarcastic words, her huge, golden eyes reproaching him before she closeted herself in the small room. Sinking down onto the toilet seat, Kit sniffled and, grabbing a thick wad of toilet tissue, she noisily blew her nose. Well, she'd certainly gotten herself into one doozy of a mess this time, but the difference was that this time she'd been the one to get hurt as well. And hurt a lot. But her pain wasn't over yet. Through the door she heard Victoria St. Clair's voice as clearly as if the woman were standing directly in front of her.

"You know, Stephen, the least you could have done before you left me to her tender mercies was to warn me that she was *that* Kit Mallory!"

And then Stephen St. Clair laughed.

SLOWLY KIT SANK to the sand, drawing her knees up against her chest protectively, and just huddled there, feeling suddenly very lost and very, very alone. Kit buried her head in her arms, a glistening, solitary tear tracing a forlorn little path down her cheek.

CHAPTER THREE

"HAND ME THAT screwdriver. No, no! The Phillips head."
Silently Kit handed it up to Todd, hiding a smile at his irritated expression. "Dammit, Kit, you're supposed to be
the electrical expert, not me! Why aren't you up here?"

Kit tilted back her head, batting her long, dark brown
lashes at him, quite happy not to be perched at the top of
a decidedly shaky-looking ladder. "But you're the man,
Todd," she informed him sweetly. "And this is a man's
job."

Todd snorted in disbelief. "That's a first! Since when
have you acknowledged sexual differentiation in connection with vocational skills?"

"Ever since you decided to put a hole in St. Clair's
wall," she retorted smugly.

He glared down at the top of her honey-blond head,
tempted to drop something on it. "Well then, just don't
plan on taking any of the credit for this hole. I think St.
Clair will be very pleased with my idea for a warning light
and an intercom system. I, for one, don't intend to have
any more lab accidents, and if a flashing red light that
alerts people to experiments in progress will do it—well, so
much the better." He turned back to the wiring. "I still
can't believe we weren't fired over yesterday's little fiasco."

"Me neither," Kit agreed fervently.

"So how about coughing up the details? All you've told
me is that you explained the situation to him." He handed

down the screwdriver and pulled a pair of wire strippers from his pocket, his concentration focused on the electrical connections in front of him. "You must have done one fast number on the iceman, that's all I can say."

Kit winced at the nickname, glad he wasn't looking at her. Her bright red cheeks would really have given him something to comment on. And then some. "I've changed my mind, Todd. He's no iceman, believe me! More like a volcano—dormant one minute and in active eruption the next!"

Todd twisted around on the ladder to look down at her, his black eyebrows raised in mild astonishment at her vehemence. "Do tell."

"He never actually fired us," she managed to mumble, aware she had said too much. Todd's sharp gray eyes tended to see much more than she was comfortable with. "I mean, he didn't precisely say the words, but that doesn't mean he still can't."

Todd's mouth twisted sardonically. "Would you care to elaborate on that cryptic little explanation?"

"No."

Todd clambered down from the ladder and picked up the light fixture, eyeing her resignedly. "What happened this time, Kit? Did it, by any chance, have something to do with yesterday's fire engines and alarm bells? Hmm?"

"Darn it all, Todd, why must you always assume the worst?" Kit demanded heatedly, squirming at the accuracy of his guess.

"Because I know you," he replied simply, a warm gleam softening his eyes. "But if you say not . . ." he said lightly, pinning her with a quizzical look. Seeing the mutinous expression on her face, he shrugged, his attention shifting once again to the lamp in his hands.

With an ease Kit envied, Todd regained the top step of the ladder, leaning precariously toward the wall. "By the way, what did you do to my name tag? It's bent into more angles than I thought existed."

This time there was no hiding the bright rush of color in her cheeks, and Todd, after several mute seconds had ticked by, glanced at her, his eyes sparking with sudden interest. "You were saying?" he asked curiously, an eyebrow quirking upward.

Refusing to answer immediately, Kit carefully considered the mischievous imp who controlled her fate. Obviously the creature had a very warped sense of humor and a high disregard for fair play. Might it be possible to request a replacement? she pondered seriously. With some regret she shook her head. Knowing her luck, she'd end up going from the frying pan into the fire. Better to stick with the familiar. "The pin got snagged on something and I had a little bit of trouble unsnagging it," she finally explained with great reluctance.

"Snagged," Todd repeated, his eyes never moving from her delicately pink face. He tilted his head thoughtfully to one side. "Why do I get the distinct impression that I'm missing something here?"

Forcibly restraining herself from kicking the ladder out from under him, Kit growled, "Your name tag got caught on a shirt. Okay? Just—a—shirt." At the glimmer of amusement in Todd's face, she added grudgingly, "I guess I lost my temper."

"Well, I guess so! And took it out on my poor name tag. That was nice of you. Feel free to replace it anytime," he suggested with mock-indignation. Finishing the connections for the light, he inserted the final screws. "At least it explains the piece of silk I found stuck in the clasp. I suppose if I'd caught the damn thing on an expensive shirt like that, I'd have been a bit peeved myself...." At Kit's strangled squeak Todd stuck his head beneath his upraised arm to peer down at her puce-tinged face.

"What is it with you? You're not usually this ditsy unless you've pulled one of your more crazy—" Todd broke off, his eyes widening for an instant as a thought suddenly occurred to him. Slowly a tiny grin began to curl at the corners of his mouth, a grin he brought ruthlessly under control, as he made his tone of voice appropriately serious. "I'll tell you, kiddo, it must be nice to have the money to buy such expensive silk shirts.... What did you say, Kit?"

"Nothing!"

"Strange, though—" Todd waited until Kit's wary eyes were raised to his before commenting guilelessly, "I could have sworn the material was from a man's shirt."

Kit shut her eyes. There was a long moment of awful silence that was finally broken by a choking sort of cough. Not able to stand it a moment longer, Kit peeped up at Todd, chagrined to see him convulsed with laughter. "What's so funny?" she snapped irritably.

"You should see your face," he gasped, only regaining his composure with heroic effort. He fiddled once more with the light in his hands, his lips still twitching suspiciously. "One last thing before we end this fascinating discussion. I found some peculiar articles draped over the sink when I went to take my shower yesterday. I don't suppose you know whose they are?"

"I don't believe this," Kit groaned, wanting nothing more than to sink through the floor. Her underclothes! She'd forgotten all about them.

"I have to tell you, Kit, my imagination is going absolutely wild—torn shirts, bent name tags, alarm bells and fire engines. But what really boggles the mind is the thought of some woman running around without any underwear..."

"Oh, shut up, Todd! Just for that, you can fix the stupid light all by yourself. I'm taking a break," she barked, and stomped off with his parting shot chasing her down the hall.

"But Kit, you never told me—precisely *why* is St. Clair a volcano now instead of an iceman?"

IT WAS MUCH LATER in the day that Stephen St. Clair made an appearance outside the lab. He stood quietly for several minutes watching Todd make the final adjustments to the intercom, his eyes moving from the red globe above the door to Kit, an odd gleam flickering in his eyes. Was that amusement? Kit wondered uncomfortably.

"Clever idea, Mr. Templeton," he finally said approvingly. "I hope this will give the rest of us a fighting chance against Miss Mallory's unfortunate proclivities."

"Or, at the very least, save you a few suits, Mr. St. Clair," Kit commented wryly, regretting the remark the moment she'd said it.

Stephen's attention was instantly fixed on her, his ice-blue scrutiny sending a shock wave through the entire length of Kit's body. "Thank you for reminding me, Miss Mallory. I believe the exact tally for yesterday's debacle comes to two suits and three shirts. And you can count yourself fortunate if that's the only expense I deduct." Kit squirmed uncomfortably, not missing his subtle reference to the damage to both his office and the lab.

"Three shirts, Kit?" Todd whispered softly into her ear. "Not a blue silk one among them, by any chance?"

Stephen's laserlike regard sliced through Todd. "You have something to add, Mr. Templeton?" he asked coldly, not missing how close the younger man's mouth was to Kit's attentive ear—and finding, for some reason, that he didn't care for the intimacy it suggested. Not at all. "Miss Mallory can consider herself extremely fortunate that she wasn't fired for the mess she made in the lab yesterday. That alone—"

"Wait a minute! What did you say?" Todd cut in sharply. He turned an accusing glower on Kit's averted face. "You told me you'd explained it all to him, Kit!"

"I did, so drop it, Todd," she muttered, dismayed when he made a move toward Stephen. "Just leave it alone," she hissed urgently, grabbing his arm. "We can discuss it later."

"The hell we will!" Todd brushed off her hand and stepped forward, placing himself deliberately in front of Kit. "There seems to be some confusion here, Mr. St. Clair. Kit wasn't to blame for the accident with the powder, I was. I assumed she'd told you that. You see, without her knowing, I'd premixed the chemicals and then spilled some water into them, setting off the reaction. So if you intend to fire anyone, it should be me."

Stephen's glance shifted to Kit as she stepped out from behind Todd, a strange look deepening the intense blue of his eyes. "Commendable of you to set the record straight, Mr. Templeton." Stephen addressed Todd, but continued to hold Kit's wide gold gaze with his. "Unfortunately your gesture is misplaced. As head of Testing and Research, Miss Mallory is responsible for all the actions of her department. The fault may have been yours, but the accountability is hers alone."

"I'll tell you this—if you fire her, you'll be losing the best department head you have!" Todd declared rashly, moving a step closer to Kit, deliberately breaking the eye contact between the two of them.

"Shut up, Todd!" Kit ordered in a low voice, feeling color flooding her cheeks.

"No, I won't!" Todd glared at Stephen St. Clair, angry frustration wiping the usual good humor from his face. "Kit is brilliant when it comes to dreaming up changes and adjustments to the toys we get. You couldn't find anyone better. In the past three months, there hasn't been a single item that has passed through our section that hasn't been improved tenfold because of her.''

"So the record shows," Stephen began, only to be interrupted by a fiercely protective Todd.

"If you did a cost analysis of the situation, you'd find the price tag on her errors is far outweighed by the profitability of her refinements. And not only that but some of her so-called mistakes have actually created a few new ideas for the Development Department."

"Your loyalty is—"

"Obviously needed," Todd inserted swiftly. "I'll be the first to admit that Kit's exuberance can be a trifle overwhelming. But it's that very approach that was needed to give The Toy Company its competitive edge in today's marketplace."

"Enough, Templeton." Stephen sighed, wearily, running a hand through his hair. "You've more than made your point. Tell me, Miss Mallory, how do you do it?"

"How do I do what?" Kit asked in confusion, still a trifle stunned by Todd's spirited defense.

"How do you manage to convince everyone to champion you so passionately? Do you pay them, by any chance?"

Kit gasped at the insult, any contrition she felt for the events of the previous day instantly evaporating. "You must be joking!" she snapped.

"Well—" he shrugged carelessly, a funny little smile quirking the corners of his firm mouth "—it was a thought. You do seem to arouse a certain protective instinct in people."

"Kit . . ." Todd muttered the warning, seeing the persuasiveness of his argument rapidly going up in smoke. The fury clouding her face did not bode well for their future.

"Do you really think I'd attempt to bribe Todd into taking the fall for me?" Her hands balled into fists at her sides. She wanted nothing more than to use them where they'd count most. "You can't seriously believe he'd lie on my behalf?"

"Take a bribe?" Stephen gave a reassuring shake of his blond head. "Actually I was just being facetious about that, and I apologize. It was a cheap shot. No, Kit, I don't imagine for one minute that you'd offer a bribe, any more than I think Mr. Templeton would take one. Neither of you would be here if I supposed otherwise."

He shot a silently simmering Todd a thoughtful look. A look that saw far more than Kit did. "But lie to save your pretty hide? Actually he just might," Stephen informed her coolly. Before Kit could release the flood of irate words trembling on her lips, he added briskly, "I'm convinced he didn't lie about his culpability in this instance, however. And if he were to try it in the future—count on it, I'd know." Gray eyes met blue, an unspoken understanding passing between them.

Kit was clearly not mollified. But when she would have said more, he shook his head abruptly, ending the discussion with a dismissive gesture. "It really wasn't my intention to get into yet another argument with you, Miss Mallory. What I do want is to see you in my office."

Kit opened her mouth and then shut it again, her anger totally diffused as his words sank in. She darted an alarmed glance at Todd, not at all reassured by his grave shrug. "Now?" she asked weakly. Was he planning to fire her after all? she wondered, her heart dropping all the way down to her toes. Despite everything that had been said?

He gestured toward the bank of elevators. "If it wouldn't be too much trouble?" he requested, a hint of exasperation entering his voice.

"This makes two days in a row I've ended up here." Kit swallowed nervously when she once again stepped into Stephen's office, her eyes widening in astonishment at its perfect condition. How had he pulled that off in such short order?

"Mmm. Why do I get the impression it's going to become a habit with you?" he said from directly behind her, his hand on her shoulder, firmly ushering her into the room.

She stiffened beneath his touch, a touch that was like a hot iron burning into her skin, branding her with its heat. For an instant she shut her eyes, reliving those moments when she had fallen against him, trapped against his hard body, feeling his taut, muscular form beneath her own. It had been such a peculiar experience to be made so suddenly aware of her own femininity. And of Stephen's overwhelming masculinity, a masculinity that was at this very instant making itself felt . . .

Kit blinked in bewilderment. Was she crazy? she wondered, totally confused by her reaction. Oh, Lord, she must be. She must be going stark, staring mad to have such thoughts, when all Stephen had done was touch her. On the shoulder yet. If he were even to suspect the emotions racing through her, she shuddered to think what he'd have to say about it. Carefully Kit eased away from him, praying he wouldn't sense anything amiss, that he wouldn't pick up on the discomfiture she was struggling so hard to conceal.

"Kit?" he said quietly, a question in his voice.

"I think I'm beginning to hate this room," she said, laughing shakily. She turned wide golden eyes on him, not quite able to conceal a certain amount of dark emotion in their glittering depths. "I can't help associating it with being in trouble. First yesterday, now today." She bit her lip to control the slight quiver there and finally managed to ask in a husky voice, "I *am* still in trouble, aren't I? That *is* why I'm here?"

Stephen moved over to stand directly in front of her, one hand cupping her chin and raising it upward, the other heavy on her shoulder. He stared down into her defenseless face, a touch of compassion softening the rugged lines of his countenance. "Not exactly, Kit. But it is about time you and I got a few things straightened out between us."

She moistened her lips with the tip of her tongue, watching something flare into life deep in his eyes, darkening their irises to a rich sapphire. That was the third time today that he'd used her first name, she realized, shivering at the gentleness of his touch. "I guess we got off on the wrong foot yesterday," she murmured, glancing up at him uncertainly.

Stephen's mouth quirked humorously. "I suppose that's one way of looking at it. I just want to be sure it doesn't happen again."

Her eyes shifted slightly to encompass the room around them. "The accidents, you mean?"

Stephen nodded in agreement. "Something has to be done about that, don't you think?"

He seemed on the verge of saying more but a brisk tapping at the door prevented him. Reluctantly his hand slid away from her and he gestured to the chair in front of his desk. "Sit down, Kit," he ordered briskly, heading for the door. "That should be Miss Dobson. Let's see if the three of us can't get this whole thing cleared up."

"I found it!" Miss Dobson announced triumphantly, bustling into the room. "And they say I have no sense of direction. Pooh! Your office is right where I last left it." She paused in front of Stephen's desk, her sweet face assuming a ferocious look. "Now if you'd only keep it here for a while, instead of mixing everything all up—"

"We'll do our best," Stephen assured Miss Dobson solemnly, waving her toward a chair, and once she was settled, he seated himself. He glanced swiftly at Kit. "This morning, Miss Dobson was kind enough to give me all your files," he explained briefly, his expression suddenly unreadable. "Unfortunately when we had our conversation yesterday, I only had the—'' He hesitated. ''Well, to be perfectly frank, I only had the damage reports on you. This time I have everything I need, and we can be a trifle more accurate.'' Stephen tapped a long-fingered hand on top of the stack of papers before him, a small frown creasing his brow. ''I've studied your records at some length—''

''And...'' Kit prompted, nervous concern assailing her. Why was he stalling? Was he still considering firing her? Was that why Miss Dobson had been called in—to soften the blow? Color swiftly mounted Kit's cheekbones as suspicion crept in. Well, so much for all his kind compassion, his desire to reach some sort of amicable understanding!

''Precisely what was it you were looking for, Mr. St. Clair?'' she queried stiffly. If he thought the few paltry mistakes she'd made were justification for letting her go, he had another think coming! Let him try firing her—she'd fight him every step of the way! Kit's chin lifted proudly. ''If you're digging for more dirt, perhaps I can save you the time and trouble. Just give me an idea of the sort of thing you're looking for, and I'll see if I can't accommodate you.''

Stephen's blue gaze iced over. ''Contrary to your paranoid delusions, Miss Mallory, I'm more interested in your credentials than any dirty little tales you might have to tell.''

Kit leaned forward in her chair, her eyes flashing resentfully. ''My credentials are impeccable—''

''Which you've told me before,'' he cut in sharply. ''I'm simply attempting to—''

''So if you're looking to use that as an excuse—''

''That isn't at all what I'd—''

''Why don't you just fire me and get it over—''

''Don't tempt me!'' His voice rose a decibel. ''Because, believe me, it would be my pleasure!'' He inhaled deeply, struggling for control. "Do you think you could possibly sit quietly for just five minutes?" he demanded tautly. "That's all I ask. Just—five—minutes." Color rose ominously in his face when Kit opened her mouth to retort.

"Be—*quiet*!" he thundered, thoroughly losing his temper. Their eyes locked in battle—a flashing blue stare, boiling with rage, finally subduing the sparks flying from an infuriated tawny glare. Assured of Kit's silence, Stephen turned to the tiny woman, who had been watching their exchange with lively interest. "Now. Miss Dobson," Stephen said through gritted teeth. "If you wouldn't mind answering a few questions, we can be done with this." At her rapid nod, he continued in a tight voice, "I must admit to being a little confused on one small issue regarding the Testing and Research Department."

"And what is that, Stephen?" Miss Dobson asked cheerfully, shifting her tiny body more comfortably into the large, leather chair in front of his desk.

"Didn't I understand you to say that you'd hired a man as head of that department?" For a moment, the question hung in the air. And then Miss Dobson beamed, her nimble fingers busily tucking away stray wisps of white hair.

"Oh, yes!" she agreed brightly, her snowy head bobbing up and down. "Such a sweet young man he was at the interview. Polite, intelligent, just perfect for the job!"

"And his name?" Stephen asked, pointedly ignoring Kit's tiny exclamation of disbelief.

Miss Dobson blinked at Stephen in dismay. Then she frowned in concentration, running swiftly through a list of names under her breath. "Malcolm, Matthews, Malloy...Kurt Mallory," she finally managed to say, a pleased expression crinkling her face. "I think."

"That's *Kit* Mallory, Miss Dobson," Kit inserted swiftly, braving Stephen's wrathful glower and returning it with a defiant one of her own. Did he really think she would sit idly by while he railroaded her? Huh! "Isn't that who you meant?" she asked the tiny woman.

Miss Dobson turned toward her, a puzzled frown puckering her forehead. "You know, dear, I do believe you're right." She peered at Stephen over the rim of her glasses, smiling apologetically. "Kit Mallory. A charming young man..."

Kit struggled to suppress a grin, suddenly beginning to enjoy herself. She watched with interest as Stephen strove to conceal his exasperation from Miss Dobson and then interrupted again, not wanting him to say anything thoughtless that would hurt the poor woman's feelings. "Miss Dobson," Kit explained gently, "*I'm* Kit Mallory."

"Of course you are, my dear," Miss Dobson agreed warmly. "Charming girl, absolutely charming." Her happy expression faltered a tiny bit, realization visibly striking her. "Oh, dear," she breathed nervously, glancing rapidly from Kit to Stephen, as tiny white curls drifted down around her flushed face. "Have I made an error?"

"It's nothing serious." Stephen forced the reassurance through stiff lips. "I just wonder—precisely who was it you intended to hire?"

The change in Miss Dobson was amazing. One minute she was the dotty old lady and the next, a minicomputer, rattling off at an alarming rate the impressive string of Kit's personal statistics, educational degrees and pertinent background. "That's who I'd planned on hiring," she informed Stephen when she'd finally come to the end of her lengthy recital. She glanced at Kit, the reflection of light off her lenses giving her eyes a distinct twinkle. Or was she secretly laughing? Kit wondered. "That is you, my dear, isn't it?" she asked Kit innocently.

"Yes," Kit murmured in agreement, shooting a nonplussed Stephen an amused glance. "Those are my credentials."

"Well, then." Miss Dobson sighed in relief. "As I was saying. A charming girl, absolutely charming. And such an asset to the company, wouldn't you agree, Stephen?"

Kit supposed the strangled sound coming from her employer was agreement, but she couldn't be sure. Obviously Miss Dobson thought so, for the next instant she was out of her chair. "Now if there isn't anything else, I'll be on my way. What a dear girl you are to get the door for me." She thanked Kit effusively. "So mannerly, Stephen. You won't often find such a jewel these days."

For an instant Kit was certain she saw a gleam of shrewd intelligence in Miss Dobson's sharp blue eyes. Then it was gone, all expression safely hidden by the distorting glass of her spectacles.

"Why do I feel as if I've been hit by a hurricane?" Stephen growled, as the door closed softly behind Miss Dobson.

"And why do I always feel as if up is down and down is up after each meeting with her?" Kit responded lightly, turning to face him.

Stephen grinned, shaking his head, perplexed. "She's something else. But as usual, she is right about one thing."

Kit held her breath, not quite sure whether she was about to be insulted or complimented. "And what is that?"

"Despite everything, she hired the right person for the job. Not only is your background impressive, but I stayed up last night researching the improvements you've made since joining the firm."

"And?" Kit asked softly, not quite believing her ears.

"And Todd was quite right. Even your mistakes somehow turn into money-making ideas." His expression was very serious, his blue eyes meeting hers squarely. "Kit, I want to apologize for all the misunderstandings. It wasn't my intention to fire you when I came down to the lab today. In fact, I was going to tell you about my findings."

"Until Todd jumped into the fracas."

Stephen nodded, his brows drawing together. "He's very defensive when it comes to you," he commented, the watchful expression on his face belying his idle tone. "Quite the champion."

Kit shrugged unconcernedly. "Try thinking of it as a personality quirk. You know, rooter for underdogs, protector of the protectorless, and guardian of klutzes. It's all part of the package—nothing personal."

Stephen was very still. "Are you sure?"

Kit frowned, feeling she'd lost the drift of the conversation somewhere along the line. "Am I sure of what? That Todd has an outmoded sense of chivalry?"

"That it's nothing personal."

Kit froze. Where was he heading? she wondered suspiciously, wishing she'd paid a little closer attention to the direction in which he'd been leading them. Surely he wasn't actually implying that she . . . that Todd . . . that they'd . . . "I hope you aren't suggesting what I think you are," Kit stated frigidly.

A blond eyebrow rose arrogantly. "Todd admitted that the error in the lab was his," Stephen pointed out with cool logic. "If his mind wasn't on the job at hand because he was preoccupied with thoughts of—"

"Don't say it!" Kit warned, all five-foot-four of her bristling with aggression. "Don't you dare say it! You finally discover that I'm not the brainless idiot you thought, and so now you're looking for another scapegoat. Well, it's not going to be Todd!"

"Of course, there's nothing personal in your defense of him, is there?"

Kit couldn't miss the sarcasm. She matched it with some of her own. "Heaven forbid I might like someone I work with. Especially if I'm a woman and he's a man. Just because you can't abide the idea of being in the same room with someone of the opposite sex without making a move on her doesn't mean—"

Dark blue eyes speared her. "As I recall it, you were the one doing the moving, Miss Mallory. Do you always find it necessary to tackle a man in order to get him horizontal?"

"*Ohh!* I did not tackle you, I tripped and fell against you." At the skeptical lift of his brow, Kit's temper rose past the boiling point. "And, despite your lewd suggestions, I was *not* out to get you horizontal, vertical or even diagonal. In fact, I wouldn't have you if you were stripped naked and dipped in fourteen-carat gold!"

"A tantalizing thought—"

"And I'm not sleeping with Todd!"

There was the abrupt crash of a file-cabinet drawer from the outer office, followed immediately by the urgent clatter of a typewriter. Kit closed her eyes, groaning in appalled disbelief.

"I'm so glad you shared that bit of information with everyone." Stephen folded his arms across his chest, amusement brightening his eyes, a wide grin spreading across his face. "And I'm equally sure the rest of the office building is happy to have such a nasty piece of gossip cleared up."

"You—you—"

"You're sputtering." He took a step closer to her and grasped her shoulders, pulling her up against him, laughing softly. "Shut up, Kit."

Then he leaned forward and kissed her, his mouth warm and firm against hers.

Kit yanked away from him. "What did you do that for?" She lifted a hand to her tingling lips.

"I couldn't resist. It was my hormones," he explained with mock-earnestness. "I'm a man and you're a woman. And we are in the same room together, all alone." He shrugged, leaning closer, his warm breath caressing her face. "I couldn't help it—I had this overwhelming desire to make a move." The words were whispered softly, teasingly into her ear.

Kit felt the color slide into her face, and a strange quivery feeling started in the pit of her stomach, spreading relentlessly upward and outward. What in the world was he doing to her? She could feel his touch, the gentle graze of his lips against her temple, the delicate movement of his fingers sliding up the silky skin of her arms, the harsh pressure of his rigid thighs against the undeniably feminine curves of hers—and she shivered helplessly, completely ensnared by the unexpectedness of his assault.

She knew she should pull away, should offer some sort of protest. But Kit couldn't, she didn't want to. Her body was perfectly pliant in his arms, curving welcomingly into him, as though she belonged there.

"Please, I . . ." The breathless words escaped her lips as a husky murmur, softly stirring the air between them. Haltingly Kit's arms crept up across his broad chest until she gripped the wide expanse of his shoulders. Her head dropped back, and she raised huge, vulnerable eyes to his. "Please, we shouldn't . . ."

It was impossible to resist what was so reluctantly offered. And Stephen didn't even attempt to. He had kissed her the first time impulsively, without due thought or consideration. But this time there was firm determination in the way he drew her to him. Very slowly Stephen lowered his head toward hers, till their lips met, his mouth feathering hers with light, teasing little strokes. Gradually he increased the pressure, drawing out each kiss, prolonging the exquisite sensations, building each heated exchange upon the next. And with each passing moment, building the desire that had unexpectedly flared between them.

The buttons of her shirt gave way to his seeking hands and she trembled at the first warm brush of his fingers. His lips slid from her mouth, easing downward along the sensitive skin of her throat, nudging the material of her shirt from one rounded shoulder, nibbling at the creamy smoothness of her skin.

Kit could feel her heart pounding in her breast, and knew Stephen must also feel the frantic throb beneath his wandering mouth. She moved urgently against him, melting fluidly into his hardness, wanting the provocative caresses to go on and on.

She never heard the knock at the door. One minute she was in Stephen's arms and the next she had been set gently away from him. Her golden-brown eyes, clouded with passion, stared up at him in bewilderment. Kit licked her swollen lips. "What—" she began in confusion.

"The door," he bit out tersely, roughly. "There's someone at the door."

Slowly the desire ebbed from Kit's body, as sanity gradually returned. She cleared her throat. "Well, my guess is, it's not your mother," she muttered, desperately fighting the confusion that fogged her brain.

"Kit." Her name on his lips was half a groan, half a laugh. The knock came again. "In a minute," he called out impatiently, his impassioned eyes never leaving hers. "Damn," he muttered, reaching out for her and sweeping her shirt closed. "Would you please hold still," he demanded in exasperation. "Stop wiggling long enough so that I can do up these buttons."

She made a face at him, but held still, knowing that if he didn't fasten her shirt, it wouldn't get done. She curled her trembling fingers into a fist, aware that her body was reacting violently to the brush of his hand against her breasts. What was wrong with her? How could she allow him to get so close to her, to... A burning flush suffused her face. To allow him such an intimate exploration of her body. Never before had she felt such a violent reaction to a man and yet, with Stephen, all he had to do was touch her and she went up in flames.

Whoever was on the other side of the door was certain to know it, too. The air fairly crackled with the electricity between them. And there would be no concealing the swollen redness of her mouth or—her eyes widened as she hastily reached out and rubbed a hand across his mouth— the trace of lip gloss on his face.

Stephen gave her one more searching glance before nodding decisively and going to open the door.

"Was I interrupting, Stephen?" a soft voice asked apologetically. "I hate to disturb you at work."

"Not at all," Stephen assured the young woman waiting patiently at the door. "Come on in. Lydia, I'd like you to meet Kit Mallory. Kit, this is Lydia—"

"Stephen!" There was a tiny break in Lydia's voice, and she threw a swift, apologetic glance toward Kit. "I've got to talk to you, it's urgent! Please excuse us," she said, turning briefly toward Kit before drawing him off to one side of the room.

"Lydia, what the hell is this all about?"

"You've got to do something about your mother," the younger woman whispered fiercely. "She's ruining all our plans with her ceaseless meddling. I can't even decide the style for your tux, let alone my own dress! And the flowers! She's even changed the order I placed for those."

"Lydia, I'm sure if you'd just tell her—"

"No! She won't listen to me. Stephen, please! You've got to do something." She laid a hand imploringly on his arm. And sparkling on the third finger of that soft, white hand was a huge, glittering diamond. "Stephen, please!"

CHAPTER FOUR

"SO HE REALLY wasn't too ticked off, then? I mean, when I butted in and told him that he was wrong about you?"

Kit hesitated momentarily, wondering how much Todd had heard about her argument with St. Clair. "He was a little . . . taken aback that you'd defend me so staunchly," she finally said.

"Not surprising," Todd retorted grimly, opening the box that contained their latest project. "He probably had you pegged as an easy target and didn't expect anyone to stand up for you."

Kit squirmed uncomfortably. "Oh, I wouldn't go that far."

"Well, I would." He turned toward her with an unexpected scowl. "It's one thing for me to razz you, kiddo, but when he starts in on you—well, let's just say my sense of fair play gets offended."

Kit's golden eyes searched Todd's face, wondering uneasily if Stephen had been closer to the mark than she'd thought. Could Todd feel something for her? Something more than mere camaraderie? No, she shook her head decidedly, they were friends, that was all. There'd never even been a hint of anything more between them. He was just displaying brotherly affection. As Fredrik might. Firmly she dismissed the matter from her mind. Besides, there was something else that was of more immediate concern. "Todd, have you heard anything about St. Clair being engaged?'' she asked cautiously, hoping her voice didn't reveal her intense interest.

Todd's eyes narrowed on her. "I'd heard rumors," he replied evenly, handing over her half of the war-game pieces they were to test. "You know how it is in a place like this—nothing is sacred, especially not the boss's love life."

"You know her name?"

She could feel his intent regard. "Lydia something or other," he informed her, his gray eyes sharpening. "Why all the interest, Kit? Thinking of offering some competition?"

"Of course not," she scoffed. "I just met her on Friday, that's all. She's nice," Kit added with a hint of despair, not quite able to drop the subject. "I mean, really nice. It's not a facade, either. You know how with some people you can just tell straight off—gosh, that person is nice." She pressed her lips together abruptly, realizing she was running off at the mouth.

Todd adjusted his missile launcher an inch to the left. "So why does that bother you? Were you hoping she'd be like the Wicked Witch of the West and St. Clair would get his just deserts?"

Kit began to arrange her military targets for their war game across the width of her playing field, their locations hidden from Todd's view by a large screen. "No!" *Yes,* she groaned silently. *Then I wouldn't feel nearly so guilty about what we had been doing just before she walked in.*

She had spent a whole weekend agonizing over the incident and even now, on Monday, she wasn't feeling any better about it. How could Stephen kiss her like that when he was committed to another woman? Then, silently, Kit castigated herself. *Oh, don't be so naive! Didn't you learn anything about men from Jeffery?* Maybe all of them weren't as unscrupulous as he had been, but a certain amount of caution wasn't unreasonable.

Her brow puckered in a confused little frown. Still she would have bet her very last dollar that Stephen wasn't like that. He was too principled to lie and cheat, to lead a woman on when all along . . . when all along he was engaged to Lydia Whosit!

Kit glared blackly at her playing board. Right. And just look at how wrong she had been about good ol' Jeff. If she could make such a mistake about him, didn't that indicate that she wasn't exactly the best judge of character? After all, hadn't she initially thought Stephen was some sort of iceman? No more. No way! Not after that kiss they'd shared. Why, the man could kiss the stripes off a zebra!

"So what does Miss Paragon look like?" Todd interrupted her bleak thoughts, beginning to load his missiles into the launcher.

Kit sat back on her heels, her mouth twisting wryly at the memory. "Gorgeous. She has this wonderful creamy skin, masses of curly, auburn hair and these huge sherry-colored eyes."

"Oh, I don't know, Kit, old bean. Personally I'm rather fond of short, attractively rounded blondes with big gold eyes. How old is she?"

"Young." Kit frowned. *Too* young. "Twenty, maybe twenty-one. And she's very slender. A really gorgeous figure."

Todd grinned wickedly. "As well endowed as yours, kiddo?" he asked with a lascivious waggle of his black brows.

"Oh, shut up, Todd," Kit muttered rudely. "It's brains that count nowadays."

Todd looked doubtful. "If you say so. Does Miss Paragon have brains, too, or is she all—"

"Todd!" Kit bit the word out in exasperation, tempted to commit a first strike on his dark, rumpled head.

"Okay, okay," he said, laughing unrepentantly. "I apologize. I assume she isn't lacking in that department, either?"

"No, she has a full complement of brains." In fact the woman was perfect. "Talent, intelligence, grace, beauty." Kit paused momentarily to shake her head in disbelief at Todd. "Would you believe it? She attended Juilliard on a scholarship. What the devil she sees in St. Clair I'll never know." *Liar! Liar!* Just imagining the two of them together, their impassioned bodies intertwined, was driving her stark, staring mad. Although why it should, she didn't even want to consider.

"I know what you mean," Todd said mournfully, the keen glance he turned on an unsuspecting Kit at odds with his tone of voice. "The man is so decrepit it's pathetic."

"Decrepit!" Her head jerked up.

"It must be his money," Todd continued blithely, ignoring her exclamation. "I can't think of any other reason a woman would want to marry him. It couldn't be for sex. She'd obviously have to find that elsewhere."

"What!"

He raised wide, gray eyes to her indignant gold ones. "Well, you certainly wouldn't want to suffer his clumsy lovemaking, would you?"

"Clumsy!" Kit cried in outrage, incredulous that he could think such a thing about Stephen—the man had been anything but! "I'll have you know he's absolutely—" Kit stumbled to a stop, eyeing Todd suspiciously, and clamping her mouth firmly shut.

"Yes? You'll have me know he's absolutely—what?" he questioned innocently.

"Nothing," Kit muttered, ducking her head and returning her attention to the game before her. When would she learn to keep her big mouth shut?

"And should I assume that your knowledge—that he's 'absolutely nothing' I mean—comes from personal experience?"

"You are a class-one rat!" Kit declared heatedly. "And just for that, I intend to annihilate your army with my X-2 missiles and Z-series cannons."

Todd studied her silently for a moment, disappointed that she'd unwittingly confirmed his hunch. "Well," he told her quietly, his voice unusually serious, "be careful you don't get annihilated in return, love. It's a very dangerous game you're playing." Then he continued briskly, "Turn on the warning light while I check over these directions one more time."

"Okay, just a sec. I've still got one or two little adjustments to make here." Kit caught her tongue between her teeth, concentrating on the long, slender objects in her hand. "Why are these missiles so heavy, Todd? Is there something in them?"

"Explosives."

"What!" Kit nearly dropped the three she held in her hand, her startled gaze flashing upward to Todd's grinning face. "Would you stop joking around! I almost had a heart attack."

"Relax. It's just a small pellet to make the front of the missile a little heavier. When they land, the pellet bursts and it leaves a little round powder mark. Nontoxic, washable, et cetera, et cetera. That way, you know what's been demolished. Everything that's been marked by the powder is considered 'hit.'"

Kit wrinkled her nose dubiously. "More powder?" she questioned unhappily. "In all honesty, I've had my fill of that sort of thing."

Todd's attention returned to the directions. "This is totally different, so stop worrying. Now take the little control panel and punch in a series of strikes. When we've both got them programmed, we push the start button and sit back. The trick is, if I knock out one of your launch sites before it's been activated, you lose it. Should we give it a go?''

"If you say so.'' She'd suddenly lost her enthusiasm for the experiment. She'd never been particularly fond of war games, anyway, and this one seemed a trifle too complicated and too realistic for her taste. Imitating Todd, Kit kneeled down next to the control panel on her side of the playing field and began to push in a random sequence of numbers.

"Done?'' At Kit's nod, Todd consulted the directions one final time. "Right. Now I'll count to three and we both push on three. One, two, thr—''

"Miss Mallory—'' Kit pushed the button at the same moment she heard her name spoken in an all-too-familiar voice. No! It just couldn't be. But it was.

"Duck!'' she shrieked as Stephen strode through the door. With an agility that amazed her, he hit the floor at the precise instant that the missiles whizzed through the air. The majority of them passed harmlessly over his head, but somehow he still managed to capture an errant few in his hair and one had even smacked him in the cheek, leaving a large, round, gray mark.

With a growl, he surged upwards, his powerful forearms lifting him onto his hands and knees, so that he confronted her nose to nose. "Miss Mallory!'' he roared.

Kit swallowed. "Yes?'' she whispered weakly.

"Miss Mallory!'' he roared again. "I was under the impression you now have a warning light to prevent exactly this sort of thing from happening. Please correct me if I'm wrong!''

His face was pressed so closely to hers that Kit blinked, trying to keep her eyes from crossing. His eyes really were the most amazing color. Clear, azure blue one moment, then clouding to a deep sapphire blue the next. And his lashes—long, thick gold lashes surrounding those gorgeous blue irises . . .

"Miss Mallory!"

"Yes?" She smiled idiotically. One moment she was nose to nose with him, the next she was hauled to her feet and hustled over to the door.

"Miss Mallory has left for the day. You, Mr. Templeton, will turn on the warning light and carry on with your experiment here," Stephen tossed over his shoulder. With a little shove, he pushed Kit through the doorway and followed directly on her heels, one of the white missiles dislodging from his hair and spinning across the floor to land at Todd's feet.

"Well!" Todd whistled in fascination, a speculative eyebrow cocked upward. "Seems I'm not the only one to prefer short, attractively rounded blondes with big gold eyes. What *will* Miss Lydia have to say about that?" Then he frowned. "More to the point—what do *I* have to say about that?"

"I ABSOLUTELY, positively, categorically, and unequivocally refuse to go back up to your office for another lecture!"

Stephen continued to hustle Kit down the long hallway, ignoring her protests and the rather startled and amused expressions that his employees threw their way. "Shut up!" he growled, ignoring the elevators and heading instead toward the back of the complex. Within minutes they were outside and marching across the neatly trimmed expanse of grass toward the parking lot.

"You can't just toss me out!" Kit cried in alarm, pulling against the relentless grip he kept on her arm. "My things—my purse. I don't even have my car keys," she wailed.

He dragged her over to a sleek white Audi, unlocked the door and practically shoved her into the passenger seat.

"What—" The door banged shut on the rest of Kit's words and she had to wait for him to go around to the other side and open his door before she could continue. "You can't do this," she stated emphatically the second he was seated in the rather opulent car. "I think there's a law against it. In fact I'm certain there must be."

"How that screwed up little brain of yours can be certain of anything is beyond me," he snarled, rounding on her, his face frozen into a tight mask. "You are the most—"

"Don't start calling me names, I'm warning you, or I'll really get angry," Kit threatened rashly.

"Lady, you've got me shaking in my boots."

Her brows drew together fiercely. "You should be!"

Stephen started up the powerful engine and reversed out of the parking space. Rapidly they were moving away from the complex, headed west past Palomar Airport toward the ocean. He drove silently for a long while, finally pulling off the road once they had reached a relatively uninhabited stretch of beach. He turned off the engine and sat staring out at the water.

For a moment, Kit fought with her anger at his cavalier behavior. How dare he kidnap her like this! And in broad daylight no less. Then the depressing thought struck her—what must her coworkers be thinking? Slowly, her fury dissipated, leaving in its place a sense of helplessness and—Kit shivered, shaking her head. It wasn't attraction, she denied silently. It wasn't!

Against her will, Kit's eyes lifted to the gray mark on his clenched cheek and then upward to a white missile that still clung to the thick blond strands of his hair. Calling herself every kind of fool, she reached out tentatively, grazing the rigid bones of his jaw with her fingers.

Intense anger was still blazing in his blue eyes, and the muscles were taut beneath her touch as she gently rubbed the rough skin of his cheek. She liked the abrasive scrape of his nearly invisible whiskers on the sensitive surface of her palm, feeling the beginnings of that all-too-familiar tingle in the pit of her stomach.

"You have a mark there from the missile," she murmured apologetically by way of explanation, not able to justify continuing to stroke his lean jawline long after the small gray spot had disappeared. Her hand left his face reluctantly and crept upward toward his golden head, sliding through the thick crispness of his hair and carefully removing the final missile lodged there. Gritting her teeth against the desire that swamped her, she used every ounce of her willpower not to reveal her acute longing to him.

Stephen reached up and gripped her fingers, his head turning toward her, his blue eyes still ablaze, but this time darkening with unmistakable passion. It was his turn to touch her, his determined fingers thrusting deeply into her honey-colored hair, holding her head firmly and drawing it toward him in a slow, relentless motion. For a long moment he gazed down into her softly flushed face, his eyes touching each delicate feature. "Why?" he muttered against her mouth. And then he kissed her.

It was a kiss like no other Kit had ever experienced. At the first brush of those hard, firm lips against hers, every nerve in her body burst into instant life, a hot pulsating warmth spreading over her like quicksilver. She felt like Eve confronted with the forbidden fruit. Kit knew she should resist, but she was as helpless in the face of such overwhelming temptation as her counterpart of old. Her head, too heavy for her shoulders, fell backward and all she could do was accept his mastery of her, moving with him, her lashes fluttering downward, her mouth softening and parting beneath the onslaught of his.

How she had longed for this, dreamed of being in his arms once again. She knew it was wrong, but all that mattered at the moment was that the sensations he was arousing in her go on and on. Her arms drifted upward, encircling his neck, her hands burrowing freely into his hair, her body arching upward against him.

Kit could feel the moist tip of his tongue teasing the inside of her mouth, his breath warm and sweet. He tasted slightly spicy and she wanted to drink in the flavor of him, to savor his richness.

"Stephen," she breathed against his lips, aching to be closer to him.

With a groan, Stephen dragged his mouth away from hers, sucking the air deeply into his lungs, the eyes he turned on her burning with a hot, blue flame that scorched her with his desire. "Damn! This is a complication I really could do without," he finally said, his voice ragged. He turned away from the hurt that touched her vulnerable face, and instead stared out at the ocean. The humorless laugh that filled the car had a grating quality. "I brought you out here to talk."

"I don't think I can talk." There was a tremor in Kit's voice and she buried her face against his neck, too shattered to allow him to see her expression. She could feel the rapid pounding of his heart and knew hers echoed it. And that, more than anything else, filled her with a desperate, hopeless sense of despair.

Stephen leaned his head back against the headrest, his eyes shut. "I don't understand it," he finally said. "It happens every time with you. I start out with a firm plan in mind and after two minutes in your company, everything goes haywire." He opened his eyes and glanced down at the top of her head, a head snuggled firmly in the crook of his shoulder, and a tender smile touched his mouth. "Why *is* that, do you suppose? What is it about you that's so irresistible?"

"I'm a jinx and an imbecile—two absolutely irresistible qualities," came the muffled reply. "It's your fatal flaw."

Kit could feel his rumbling laughter against her cheek and managed a smile in return.

"Look at how late it is." He touched her shoulder so that she would look up. "The clouds are rolling in and the sun is starting to set."

Sure enough, a touch of heavenly pink was painted across the misty clouds that had begun to fill the horizon. A lone gull circled above the waves breaking on the sand, its harsh shriek borne easily on the light breeze.

"I'd forgotten—" Kit caught her lip between her teeth "—my car is still in the parking lot. I hope no one thought it strange."

"I don't think anything you do anymore can be deemed strange," Stephen said dismissively, pushing her upright and away from him. "So forget about it. Besides, we haven't had our little conversation yet. And that's something that's going to have to get done—tonight."

Without further discussion, Stephen drove them back to the office building to retrieve her belongings. Kit shivered when she saw the parking lot completely deserted aside from her lonely little car. How must that have looked to all the other employees? It might not particularly concern Stephen, but she didn't like the idea of people gossiping about her. And gossip they would!

"Come on," he ordered tautly, seeing her expression. "Let's get your things. Then we're going out to dinner."

Kit didn't even attempt to argue. One look at his set face was enough to convince her it would be fruitless.

THE RESTAURANT Stephen chose was just a few blocks from Kit's duplex and was something of a landmark in Carlsbad. "I've never been here," he commented, parking outside the old Victorian structure. "But I've been meaning to give it a try."

"Oh, you should like it, it's really nice." Kit forced an enthusiastic note into her voice, striving to overcome the

stilted atmosphere between them. "I've been here before."

"And it's still standing?" came the dry comment.

Kit smiled sweetly, forcibly restraining herself from
knocking him over the head, but unable to prevent a hint
of sarcasm from creeping into her voice. "Don't worry.
They've recently done it over."

Stephen's eyes gleamed brightly with humor at her reply, and after a moment, a small smile parted Kit's soft
mouth, and her twinkling eyes met his in shared amusement. "Truce?" he suggested with a quirk of his eyebrow, and at Kit's nod he ushered her through the front
door.

"Look at all the natural woodwork," she murmured,
when they entered the lobby, admiring the soft, plush
colors that complemented the warm wood flooring and
window trim. "It was built a hundred years ago as a private residence and at some point was turned into a restaurant. They've done a wonderful job remodeling it. It's so
elegantly modern on one hand, and yet they've still managed to retain and accent the old-world grandness of the
place."

The dining area was a huge circular room in soft peach,
cream and forest green with large picture windows looking out on the attractive little shops of Carlsbad. Little is-
lands filled with large green plants were strategically placed
around the dining area, giving the illusion of privacy as
well as adding a charming accent to the room. On one side
a doorway led to a lovely glass-enclosed veranda and it was
there that the hostess led them.

"Your waitress will be with you in a moment," the attractive woman informed them as they were seated at a
small, secluded table. "In the meantime, we have quite an
extensive wine list you may wish to look over. Our spe-
cialties are the fresh fish dishes, and the pasta is home-

made." With a bright smile she handed them menus and left.

Kit stirred uncomfortably, suddenly and acutely aware of being relatively alone at an elegant restaurant with her employer—a man who not thirty minutes earlier had been making passionate love to her, and she to him. A man, moreover, engaged to marry another woman. Kit nibbled on her lower lip. How could she have allowed herself to forget that fact?

"Have you any recommendations?" Stephen asked quietly, as though sensing her apprehension and giving Kit time to slowly relax.

She peeked up at him from beneath long, brown lashes, catching her breath at the sight of the large man across from her. Why did he have to affect her so? He was so calm and self-assured, the expression on his sharply defined face faintly quizzical, the gaze from his blue eyes cool and steady. And yet some deep, hidden part of her was screaming at her, warning her of danger. This man is trouble, a small voice was saying. All you've worked for, all you've learned from that fiasco with Jeffery is going to be jeopardized if you aren't very, very careful.

"Yes, I have a recommendation," Kit announced rashly, struggling to maintain a brave front. For once she was going to listen to her instincts and forget the rest. "I recommend that from now on you start remembering that I'm your employee, and keep your hot little hands to yourself." From somewhere close behind her came a loud crash, and Kit jumped in her seat, her startled eyes widening.

"The busboy," Stephen murmured negligently, flipping open the menu and serenely beginning to peruse it. "I do believe he found your recommendation rather...novel."

Kit swallowed, feeling the color creeping up into her cheeks. "Try the cioppino," she managed in a rather strangled voice. "It's excellent."

The wine Stephen ordered was precisely what Kit needed and it wasn't until she had swallowed two full glasses that she felt able to raise her eyes from the surface of the table and dart several quick glances around the room. And it wasn't until she was nearly finished with her own exquisitely flavored pasta *al pescatore* that she could actually meet the tiny glitter in Stephen's eyes with anything approaching equanimity.

"You realize of course that this can't continue any longer."

The quiet words dropped between them, followed instantly by Kit's fork, a large pink shrimp and several fat, creamy noodles. Her worried gaze flew to his suddenly serious face and she cleared her throat nervously. "What can't?" she managed to ask, unable to conceal the touch of panic in her voice.

"The situation at work," he stated gently, leaning slightly toward her. "So far, I'm the only one who's really been adversely affected by the—" he hesitated briefly, struggling for the right words "—by the rather unfortunate side effects of your experiments."

"Well, and Todd, too."

Stephen inclined his head a trifle impatiently. "And Todd. But I really think—"

"And Mrs. Enright," Kit hastened to add, determined to be painfully honest. "You know, with the skateboard and the sod."

Stephen's voice hardened perceptibly, a harried look darkening his eyes. "All right! I stand corrected. Myself, Todd and Mrs. Enright have been placed in some unfortunate situations because of—"

"And your mother," she murmured meekly.

"Kit!"

The busboy approaching the table to remove their dinner plates did an abrupt about-face.

Stephen ran a hand distractedly through his hair, the muscles jerking in his rigidly held jaw. "What I am trying to say, if you will let me," he bit out through clenched teeth, "is that, so far, your accidents have been fairly harmless. But what if Miss Dobson had been the one to wander in on one of them and you hadn't been taking the proper precautions?"

It was obvious that the possibility hadn't occurred to Kit, for dismay was clearly written across her expressive face. She could well imagine the results if that dear soul had lost her way in the lab—and it wasn't a pretty picture. "I'm sorry! I didn't—"

"You didn't think," Stephen finished for her. His eyes revealed a hint of sympathy, but his voice remained stern. "That's your whole problem in a nutshell, Kit. You don't think." He studied her downcast eyes and the slight tremble of her soft mouth and found he had to force the hard tone in his voice. "You're not a child anymore. You're an adult with adult responsibilities. And one of those responsibilities as an employee of The Toy Company is to maintain a safe work environment for those around you. To see to it that the experiments you conduct are done carefully and safely."

"Are you firing me?" Kit asked painfully, her eyes searching his face for some hint of his inner thoughts.

He shook his head impatiently. "No, of course not. Haven't we been through that already?"

"That was before—" She stopped abruptly, wondering why on earth she was bothering to remind him about the missiles. He'd already said he wasn't going to fire her. "You're right," she acknowledged quietly. "I'd like to blame my carelessness on a surplus of enthusiasm, but I guess that would be a cop-out. I haven't thought things through the way I should have and there's no excuse for it. I'm sorry," she added sincerely.

Kit's softly worded apology affected him more than he might have wished and Stephen strove to keep that fact from her. "Your career means a lot to you, doesn't it?" he asked instead, realizing that he was curious as to the reason.

Kit nodded. "Yes. It really does," she agreed simply.

"Why?"

"Why?" she repeated, slightly taken aback, never before having had to put it into words. She thought for a moment before responding. "I guess because it's so much fun. Every day is a new challenge, a new opportunity to take someone's idea and change it just a little. To—to add my stamp to it." Kit leaned forward, her eyes brilliantly gold, glowing with an inner spark. "Maybe some people think it's silly—playing with toys. But I see it as helping children develop their imaginations, stimulate their sense of curiosity about how things work and relate to one another. Maybe they'll even learn something new, and be excited enough to try to learn something more."

"Is that all?" Stephen teased, when her words finally came to a halt.

Kit sat back with a self-conscious smile. "You did ask," she pointed out. "And you? How did you get involved in the business?"

"Actually I came upon it accidentally." He laughed when he saw the grin Kit was trying to hide. "No, no, not that sort of accident! Shortly after I graduated from college, I saw an ad in the newspaper that really intrigued me. It said something like, 'Create those wonderful toys you dreamed of as a youth, but could never buy in any store. Only the true child at heart need apply.' It turned out to be an elderly man, Smitty, who owned his own toy company and wanted to retire."

"And you bought it?" Kit asked, intrigued.

Stephen shook his head, his eyes gleaming mysteriously. "Oh, he had no intention of selling it."

"Then what?" she demanded, his story capturing her imagination.

"He wanted to find just the perfect person—someone who had the ability to dream like a child, but who also had the skills to turn those dreams into reality—to inherit the business."

"And that was you?"

"Don't sound so astonished," he retorted with mock indignation. "Smitty selected me out of hundreds of applicants, maybe thousands. He's now happily retired in La Jolla, living off his share of the stock dividends."

Kit sat back, blinking in amazement. "That's incredible." Then she eyed him suspiciously. "Is that true or did you make it up?" To her intense frustration, Stephen sat back, folding his arms across his chest, an enigmatic little smile on his face.

Kit frowned at him. "Impossible man! Just for that you'll have to answer another question," she informed Stephen. "Only this time you'll have to be honest."

His golden eyebrows winged upward. "I didn't realize we were playing that sort of game." He lowered his voice suggestively. "A little truth or dare, Kit? And if I were to choose the dare?"

To her amazement, Kit found she was actually considering it. What sort of dare would she challenge him with, if he refused to answer her question truthfully? A delicate flush tinted her face as the most deliciously erotic suggestions leaped to mind. And Stephen, darn him, knew precisely how wayward her thoughts had become.

"Tsk, tsk," he whispered in a husky voice. "What would your mother say to such naughty ideas?"

"That it was about time, probably," Kit muttered, shooting him a disgruntled look. How did he manage to do it—make her feel so flustered and jumpy? What she needed was to have him at a disadvantage for a change, to put some distance between them, get some breathing space

for herself. And she knew just the question to do it!
"Well," she goaded him. "Are you going to take me on,
or not?"

"All right, Kit," Stephen agreed resignedly. "You're
obviously dying to ask, so shoot."

"Why do you have it in for career women? What do you
have against us?"

Well, if it had been her intention to get his back up, she
had just succeeded. Royally. The shutters slapped down
over his expression with a bang, the warm blue of his eyes
freezing into an arctic wasteland. Kit had to restrain herself from bolting from the table and running willy-nilly out
into the night. "Well?" a suicidal voice demanded, and she
jumped, realizing the words were coming from her.

"That's the second time you've accused me of that.
Would you mind telling me where you got such a preposterous idea?" he asked tightly.

Kit's eyes narrowed speculatively, looking at the nervous way his fingers repeatedly adjusted the position of the
silverware. "Is it?" she demanded in turn, suddenly serious. "Is it really such a preposterous idea?" It was a puz-
zle that had been nagging at her subconscious for a long
time. And while she had originally asked the question to
stifle the growing attraction between them, she now realized that she wanted to hear his answer, wanted him to explain his reasoning to her. For there was an instinctive
surety, deep down inside, that told her she wasn't mistaken about this.

"Yes," he snapped, his fingers clenching on the table.
"I have nothing against women in the workplace. I'd be
crazy if I did."

"Then why did you want a man for my position?" Kit
asked in as nonthreatening a way as she could manage.

For a moment, he appeared to be nonplussed and then
he shrugged irritably. "I suppose because I wanted someone in there permanently. Someone I could rely on not to

suddenly drop their career the minute a suitable husband came along.''

Kit struggled to quell her own growing annoyance. ''Marriage does not necessarily preclude a career, Stephen,'' she answered, his first name leaving her lips quite naturally. ''There are lots of women who are very successful at their careers, and yet still manage to marry and raise a family.''

''Then they shouldn't!'' he hissed acridly, the words out before he could stop them.

There was a moment of stunned silence and Kit wondered who was more surprised by the scathing statement, Stephen or herself. The disconcerted horror on his face was almost comical.

''I—I—'' he stammered, for the very first time not in command of a situation.

''Stephen, why?'' Kit probed gently, her soft eyes reflecting her concern. ''There has to be a reason for your attitude...''

His faced closed over, and once again he was the coolly confident executive. ''I'm sorry, Kit, I don't know why I said that. I certainly don't believe it.''

Kit shook her head impatiently. ''If you didn't believe it, at least on a subconscious level, you wouldn't have said it. Stephen—''

''What about you?'' he interrupted, the gleam in his eyes warning her that he wasn't going to give away any more of himself. Instead he was on the attack. ''How old are you, twenty-five, twenty-six?''

''Twenty-five,'' Kit admitted, a little bewildered. ''But I don't see what that has to do with—''

''Old enough to be married and producing a few kids of your own,'' he pressed peremptorily. ''So why aren't you?''

Her mouth tightened, an angry sparkle warming the gold in Kit's eyes. "You're evading the subject, trying to put me on the defensive. We weren't discussing my—"

"We were discussing marriage and career women and how the two affect job performance," he retorted with deadly precision. "Surely that's something that directly concerns you. Tell me, Kit—" he leaned forward, pinning her with his hard, blue stare "—how do marriage and children fit into *your* career plans?"

CHAPTER FIVE

KIT MOISTENED her suddenly dry lips. Did she want a career *and* marriage and children? Oh, Lord, what was she to say to that? No matter how she responded, it was a no-win situation. There was a brief silence before she finally spoke, her voice strained and slightly husky. "You're beginning to sound like my parents," she observed quietly, in an attempt to stall for time. "They've been asking the very same thing for the past two years."

"On your back, are they?" Stephen goaded lightly, a teasing smile drawing the tension from his face. Visibly he began to relax, gesturing at her to continue. "You're skating around the question, but I'll be generous."

Meaning *she* hadn't been when the shoe had been on the other foot? Kit wrinkled her nose at him, and then decided to answer candidly. "They're beginning to hint that I'm over-the-hill. Which, admittedly, is getting to be a bit of a strain, since I hear it on nearly every visit. I think they live in eternal hope that someday I'll see the light and settle down to blissful domesticity—like Fredrik and Anne, my brother and sister-in-law."

She shook her head in confusion. "And those two are just about as bad as my parents. I can't understand why my brother is in such a hurry to see me married." Kit looked at Stephen curiously. "If you had a younger sister, would you take such an intense interest in her marital status? Would it matter all that much to you?"

She didn't know precisely what she'd said that was so terribly wrong. But it was clear she'd said something Stephen had taken exception to. His face went absolutely white, his eyes flaming briefly, then going strangely flat. Before she had time to react, he answered her.

"I think it's only natural for an older sibling to feel a certain amount of responsibility for a younger. Especially when it's a big brother and a little sister," he commented gruffly. "Surely they only want you to be happy?"

"Perhaps," she conceded, feeling a little more hesitant about airing her views after his peculiar reaction. "But happy by *their* standards, not by mine." Then promptly forgetting discretion in the face of her growing indignation, she added, "I'm supposed to go home this weekend. Take a guess why."

Relieved that she was no longer watching him quite so closely, Stephen took his time replying. He studied the soft beauty of her flushed face, the brilliant flash of gold sparkling in her heated gaze, and felt a tinge of sympathy for her. He took a stab at the answer. "They have a man all lined up and ready to go?"

Kit gave an ironic nod. "Clever you. Don't misunderstand, there's nothing wrong with Jesse, he's very nice."

"But you don't want to marry nice," Stephen said, hazarding a guess.

Hadn't he caught on yet? Was he so bound by his own prejudices that he couldn't even see that others might want something different from life? Kit threw him a disgusted look. "Why do people always assume that a single woman's sole goal in life is to marry? I mean, if it happens, it happens, but I'm not feeling particularly desperate! And if it doesn't happen—tough!"

She managed to make him blink with that rather definite statement. "Er—what about children?" Stephen asked hesitantly, wondering if he was about to step on another conversational land mine. Their discussions certainly seemed to have a life-threatening quality. "Or are they a no-go as well?"

Kit leaned back as the busboy cautiously approached to remove their dishes. "You needn't be married to have children," she informed him with a carefully cultivated, and totally transparent, sophistication. "Many women find it preferable to just have a baby and avoid the complications of marriage." The busboy gawked at her as he grabbed for her plate, his eyes bulging with avid curiosity.

As he noted the young boy's fascination with their conversation, a wicked grin began to curl Stephen's broad mouth. "Do you have a lot of experience in that field, my dear?" he asked, his deep voice laced with brazen humor. "Or were you merely vetting potential candidates?"

"Perhaps some coffee first?" The busboy's adolescent voice cracked in midsentence.

The breath exploded furiously from Kit's lungs, and one tawny-eyed glare from her dangerously narrowed eyes was enough to send the hapless boy scampering back toward the kitchen. Next she turned her scorching gaze on an openly laughing Stephen, sputtering, "You did that deliberately! You know perfectly well that I'd never—that I'm not—"

Stephen raised his hands as though warding off her anger. "You started this provocative line of discussion, I was just trying to help out."

"You may think this is some kind of joke, but I don't." Kit leaned toward him, her delicate brows drawn together over still glittering eyes. "What I need, if you would only listen to me, is my job. I don't want to be constantly on guard with you—afraid that at the least little slipup, I'll be out the door. Nor, if I do eventually marry, do I want to be terrified that you'll fire me, simply because you don't approve of working wives and mothers."

"I'm sorry, Kit," he apologized gently. "I know you think I'm taking all this very lightly, but I really am trying to understand your side of things.'' His mouth tightened momentarily. ''If someday you decide to marry, you'll still have your job. I promise I won't invent an excuse to force you out.'' His indigo-blue eyes seemed to singe her. ''But I can't say I'll be terribly happy about it.''

''*Why?*'' The single word burst from her. ''Stephen, please! You can't just make such sweeping pronouncements without giving me your reasons!''

Kit didn't think he was going to answer her, but then very quietly, a world of pain in his voice, he admitted, ''Because I've seen what that sort of arrangement can do. And I hope never to see it again.''

Their coffee and dessert arrived at just that moment, preventing Kit from pursuing the subject any further. It also gave her an opportunity to mull over Stephen's words. What had he been referring to? she speculated, peeping at him from beneath her lashes. Could something in his background have given him such an intensely negative view of career women? It wasn't an unreasonable conclusion, after all. Not if he had known someone who had been dedicated to her job to the exclusion of everything else, including her children. His mother, perhaps?

''Kit, I've been thinking,'' Stephen interrupted her thoughts abruptly. ''Perhaps part of your trouble at work is because of the pressure your parents are bringing to bear. Maybe it's bothering you just enough to distract your attention from your job.''

At Kit's indignant sputter, he waved her down. ''I'm not trying to cause you any trouble! I just thought ... Listen, I have an idea.'' He stirred his coffee for a moment before lifting his intent gaze to hers and suggesting lightly, ''Why don't I go with you this weekend to visit your parents.''

''Wha—?'' Kit started in surprise, a caramel-covered chunk of snicker pie plopping from her fork onto the tablecloth.

Stephen's lips twitched at her softly groaned imprecation, gallantly struggling to suppress the bark of laughter
that fought to escape his throat as he watched her vain ef-
forts to slip the elusively gooey mound back onto her plate.
"Oh, yes," he murmured in a strangled voice, his blue eyes
suspiciously bright. "The more I think about it, the better
I like it. Why don't you take me with you this weekend?
I've just got to—I mean, I'd just love to meet your parents."

This did not sound good. Not good at all. Kit frowned
darkly, attempting to analyze just what was going on behind his innocent expression. "I don't know what clever
little scheme you've got hatching in that equally clever
brain of yours, but you can forget it," she stated categorically. "I'm not letting you anywhere near my parents."

"Why not?" Stephen asked in wounded surprise. "I
could help your cause."

Kit snorted. "More likely provide reinforcements for
theirs!" She shook her head emphatically, not in the least
impressed by his little-boy-lost expression, even more
chary when he abruptly changed tactics.

"What would your parents do if you brought home a
man you were interested in?" Stephen interrogated her
with all the verve and skill of a trial lawyer.

"Take out a full-page ad in the newspaper," she responded promptly.

Stephen chuckled his appreciation. "I'm trying to be
serious and offer you a way out of your dilemma and all
you can do is make jokes." Her mouth flew open. Here she
was being deadly earnest—something he couldn't be for
more than two seconds straight—and *he* was accusing *her*
of— He smoothly inserted his question before she could
gather her wits sufficiently to dispute the point. "Would
it get them off your back?"

Kit frowned dubiously, momentarily forgetting her annoyance and giving careful consideration to his question.

"I'm not sure," she replied uncertainly. "They'd probably ask a lot of questions, make a few sly comments and
demand a weekly progress report but aside from that—"
She shrugged, eyeing him sharply. "But I still don't—"

"The point is, they'd let up on you, right?" he asked,
striving not to let his amusement color his voice.

Slowly Kit nodded. "I guess they would. But Stephen,
what does that have to do with—"

"Everything," he said, cutting her off firmly. "If you
bring me home with you, and introduce me as, say, your
very good friend, I have a feeling it might take care of your
more immediate problems in that direction."

Grimly Kit shook her head at his confident expression.
"You can't. You seem to be forgetting one very important, very vital detail." At his raised eyebrows, she asked
pointedly. "What about Lydia?"

Stephen shrugged carelessly, brushing her words aside
as unimportant. "The wedding's weeks away."

Kit glared at him, her mouth falling open. "Well, I
never!" she gasped.

"Look, Kit," he sighed. "You're making a big deal
about nothing."

"Nothing?" she choked out in amazement, wondering
if Lydia would see it quite that way.

"I don't see what the problem is here. I'm not propos-
ing marriage—"

"That might prove a little awkward!"

"It simply occurred to me that if your parents think you
have a love interest, maybe they'll leave you alone."

Kit shook her head again, the doubt clear in her face. "I
don't know. I don't like it."

Stephen rolled his eyes in exasperation. "For a supposedly bright woman, who's supposedly plagued by matchmaking parents, you certainly are slow to take advantage
of a helping hand."

"I suppose that depends on whose helping hand," Kit retorted a trifle tartly. Stephen's cool, blue eyes were leveled at her, and unable to withstand the steady gaze, her eyes dropped from his. "Sorry," she muttered. "That was uncalled for."

"Kit." Reluctantly she raised her head, forcing herself to face him. "What do you have to lose?" His voice was softly persuasive, as if he didn't realize how much she did stand to lose. "We visit your parents this weekend. 'Surprise, Mom and Dad, meet Stephen, my—wink, wink—good friend.' For two days, Mom oohs and ahhs. Dad asks serious questions like, 'are you employed?' and 'what's your golf handicap?'"

Kit couldn't prevent the gurgle of laughter that bubbled up. "And then?" she managed to ask.

"We take our leave, not having made any real commitments or promises in front of them. Mom and Dad are tickled pink and you're off the hook." He lifted his brows inquiringly, as though not seeing what could possibly be wrong with his suggestion.

"You mean, off the hook temporarily," Kit inserted contrarily.

"So it's temporary." Stephen waved her arguments aside with a negligent hand. "It's better than nothing, wouldn't you say?"

Kit nodded grudgingly, her golden eyes studying him warily. "And just what do you get out of all this? Or are we simply feeling altruistic this evening?"

"Oh, it won't be free of charge," he informed her softly, suggestively, enjoying the look of affronted fury that spread across Kit's face.

"Forget it! I'll have you know that I have no intention of—"

"Shut up, Kit," he said, his teasing grin taking some of the sting out of his words. "What I want from you is a promise that you'll clean up your act at work. Maybe you're trying too hard to succeed, putting too much pressure on yourself. And maybe if I take some of that pressure off, by helping you on the home front, you can get your mind back where it belongs. On your precious career. Are we in agreement?''

At her tentative nod he pushed back his chair and pulled out his wallet, tossing several bills down on the table. Kit stood with a deep sigh. ''Why do I get the feeling I'm going to regret this?'' she asked resignedly.

''You won't,'' he promised, with more confidence than clairvoyance.

And to the eternal relief of the busboy, they left the restaurant.

WELL, what was she going to do? She couldn't just go along with him like some helpless ninnyhammer! Where was her willpower, for heaven's sake? In the cold light of day, without the romantic atmosphere of a golden sunset, a candlelit dinner and several glasses of potent wine, it was impossible to delude herself any further. She was strongly attracted to Stephen St. Clair. A very improper, if not dangerous attraction, true, but there nonetheless. And, in weakly giving in to his plans for the weekend, she was courting disaster.

What would she do if he were to kiss her again? Even knowing about Lydia, even with the overwhelming guilt that knowledge caused her, she was incapable of resisting his touch. A dark, painful blush crept into her cheeks as she remembered in vivid detail her impassioned responses to his lovemaking.

''Miss Mallory.'' Kit fumbled with the control box for the Tarantula Terror, accidently switching two thin wires. Nuts! What was he, psychic or something? she wondered in embarrassed exasperation, hoping he wasn't equally as psychic when it came to knowing the precise nature of her thoughts. And why, she asked with an inward sigh, did he have to harass her every waking moment? When he wasn't busy confusing her daydreams, there he was, managing to confuse her in person.

A sudden possibility struck her. Was fortune actually going to smile on her for a change, and have him cancel out for the weekend? Perhaps he had had a few twinges of guilt as well.

She peered hopefully up at his bland face. "Yes, Mr. St. Clair?" she asked as sweetly as she could manage. "You wanted to see me?"

A hint of a smile touched his broad mouth. "Actually I wanted to see this fellow here." He gestured toward the Tarantula Terror and quirked an eyebrow. "Was there something I should be seeing you about?"

Darn him! she thought with a prick of irritation. He knows perfectly well what I'm hoping and thinks it's funny. Well, just let him get a load of her matchmaking relatives—he won't be smiling quite so widely then! More likely he'll be heading for the hills as fast as his size twelves will take him.

"You don't mind?" he asked. Kit looked at him blankly for a minute before realizing that he was waiting patiently for her permission to examine the spider, the look in his eyes daring her to protest.

"Please. Be my guest," Kit offered graciously, lowering her eyes to conceal the hint of mockery they contained. "Be careful, though. He bites."

"Taught him one of your tricks, did you?" The comment was so softly spoken, Kit almost missed it. By the time she had opened her mouth to deliver a scathing retort, he had turned his attention back to the automaton. "I must say these spiders are wonderfully hideous," he commented, gingerly lifting one of the huge, hairy creatures and shuddering delicately. He carefully moved one of the long, spindly legs. "What exactly will it be able to do when you're done with it?"

A militant gleam appeared in Kit's eyes and her jaw had a distinctly belligerent jut. "Attack," Kit stated succinctly.

Todd stepped hastily forward and took the spider from Stephen, shooting a quick, warning glance at Kit. "Well, in a manner of speaking, that is," he said, attempting to downplay Kit's words. "Naturally he'll crawl. He wouldn't be of much use if he couldn't. And bite."

Kit bared her teeth in a rough semblance of a smile. "Yes, his mandible is really quite functional and he's been given a nice, strong grip. Once the remote is connected, all I'll need to do is push a button and he'll snap away. Why don't you demonstrate for Mr. St. Clair, Todd?"

"Yes, please," Stephen insisted with a chuckle. "I'm all eyes."

"It's a little difficult to show you without the remote, but you can at least see which parts are movable," Todd explained, demonstrating the spider's capabilities. "You see where he has this nasty little opening between the jaws?" He glanced up at an attentive Stephen. "Eventually he'll be able to shoot out a white, sticky substance, but we still don't have that quite right. I think in the movie it's supposed to be some sort of acid."

"I'm looking forward to experimenting with that," Kit murmured, Stephen's sudden scowl eliciting a winning smile from her. "Although, there are still a couple of bugs we need to work out." She paused to see if he had picked up on her quip and, reassured by the twitch of his lips, added, "And we're considering one or two little surprise additions. Aside from that, I think it's coming along nicely."

Stephen nodded in satisfaction. "Webber Films should be quite pleased with this. They're very anxious to begin production, but obviously, they can't until these little guys are completed." His narrowed eyes fell on Todd. "I'd still like to take a look at the actual progress reports, Mr.

Templeton, so that I can keep them apprised of the situation." He shot Kit a warning glance when she would have opened her mouth to protest, continuing to address Todd. "Would you get those for me?"

Todd hesitated for an instant, his speculative gray eyes flickering from Stephen to Kit and back again. Then he shrugged, replying easily, "Sure thing, Mr. St. Clair. I'll have them for you in a jiffy."

Kit sent Stephen a withering look. "What was that for?" she snapped at him the moment the door had closed behind Todd. "I just sent you a copy of the progress report. Or should I assume that was a deliberate maneuver to get Todd out of the room?"

"You should. I didn't think you wanted Mr. Templeton to overhear the details of our little rendezvous this weekend." He raised his eyebrows upward quizzically. "Or did you?"

"It is *not* a rendezvous," Kit objected heatedly, her eyes reflecting the panic his suggestive words evoked. Jeffery had caused her more than a little heartache when she'd finally learned the truth about him. But instinctively, she knew it was nothing compared to what she'd experience with this man—if she allowed the situation to continue. "I've changed my mind. I'm not going!"

Stephen shook his head firmly. "Well, I have not changed mine. After this weekend you'll have no excuse for not keeping your mind on your job." He sighed when she would have protested further, taking her shoulders in a light grip and giving her a little shake. "Kit, we've already been through this and for some reason, you're trying to blow this whole thing out of proportion. If your parents ease up on you, and that in turn enables you to be a little more conscientious at work, then why not let me help you?"

Kit glared up at him, drawing away from his warm grasp. "Because I don't want your help," she cried in frustration. "It's a mistake taking you to meet my parents. I know it is. Somehow it's all going to backfire into a horrible disaster. I can see it now."

Stephen couldn't suppress a smile at her words and nodded his head. "Knowing you, you're probably right," he agreed. "But I really don't see that we have any other choice. I need an employee who's going to do a proper job, and you need a break from matchmaking parents." He studied her mutinous expression and set his jaw determinedly. "Enough, Kit! Now tell me where you live."

His tone brooked no further defiance and, reluctantly, Kit gave him the requested information. "Pasadena."

"In that case I'll pick you up at nine-thirty. I want to get us there a little before noon and I can't guarantee how long it will take to get through the traffic outside Santa Ana." And with that he was gone.

"Where's St. Clair?" Todd demanded a few moments later, annoyance sharpening his voice. He thumped a thick folder onto the table. "I thought he wanted to see this stuff."

"I guess he changed his mind," Kit muttered, bending hastily over the control box to avoid his accusing eyes.

"Or maybe he didn't really want to see it in the first place!" Todd snorted caustically, studying her bent head with an irritated frown. "What is it with you two anyway? If I didn't know better, I'd suspect there was something going on."

Kit squeezed her eyes shut, suddenly exhausted by all the confusion. Why did things have to be so complicated? "Todd, please," she finally muttered in a tired little voice, hoping against hope that he'd take the hint and leave it alone.

Instead he moved a step closer, his voice deepening with concern. "Kit, I worry about you," he murmured, laying a gentle hand on her shoulder. "I don't want to see you hurt—and an affair with St. Clair is guaranteed to hurt."

Kit pulled free of his grip, glaring up at him. "I'm not having an affair with him, nor do I intend to, so mind your own business!" she snapped. Then, realizing she was taking her aggravation with Stephen out on Todd, she touched his arm apologetically. "I'm sorry, Todd, I didn't mean to bite your head off." She sighed, offering lamely, "I—I guess I didn't sleep well last night. Do you mind if we just end this conversation?"

Todd subjected her to a brief, searching glance, and then, to her relief, dropped it, giving her braid an affectionate tug. "Hey, it's all right, kiddo," he told her cheerfully. "Running fruitless errands for St. Clair is one of my favorite pastimes. I'll tell you what. Why don't we mess around with that stuff for your spider? We can practice shooting it at each other. That should perk you up."

THE REST OF THE WEEK went surprisingly quickly. Fortunately for her nerves, Kit saw very little of Stephen. Occasionally she'd catch a glimpse of his tall, muscular figure striding down the hall, or a flash of his distinctive blond hair, but that was all. Actually it was more than enough. Those brief glimpses were all she needed to feel the nervous dread tying her stomach into knots.

By Friday night, all Kit wanted was a long, hot soak in the bathtub and some much-needed sleep. Her overnight bag was packed and ready to go, her parents had been given advance warning of Stephen's imminent arrival and all she had left to do was to wash her hair and have an early night.

To her amazement she slept dreamlessly from the minute she slipped between the cool, linen sheets until she awakened the next morning, bright sunshine filling the room. She jumped from her bed feeling rested and alert and ready to face anything. Well, almost anything. She still found the thought of playing Stephen's more-than-good friend with her family as the audience decidedly off-putting.

At precisely nine-thirty she heard Stephen's car pull up outside the duplex, and not bothering to wait for him to come to the door, she grabbed her bag and went out to meet him.

"Nervous?" he asked, once her luggage had been stowed in the trunk and they were both safely strapped into their seats.

"No," Kit lied instantly, fidgeting against the cool leather beneath her. Then, truthfully, "Yes," she sighed. "I guess I must be."

Stephen glanced at her, his hand hovering over the ignition, a sudden frown deepening the rugged lines of his face as he caught sight of her stoic expression. "They are your parents. Surely they can't be that bad."

Kit's eyes widened in dismay. "Oh, no, of course they're not. I didn't mean to give you that impression at all. It's the pretense that's got me so uptight. I've never done anything like this before."

Stephen's mouth twisted in wry amusement and he sat back against the leather seat, his hands resting on top of the steering wheel. "Believe it or not, this isn't exactly a daily occurrence for me, either." He searched her taut features for a moment longer. "You feel that you're lying to them, don't you?"

Kit nodded silently. Stephen sighed, looking out through the windshield, his expression thoughtful. "If you introduce me as I really am, as just a friend and your employer—no more, no less and no strings attached—would that make you feel more comfortable?"

Kit peered up at him uncertainly, nibbling her lip, a tiny frown puckering her brow. "Wouldn't that defeat the whole purpose of the visit?"

Stephen shook his head. "I don't think so. From what you've said about your mother, she'll have us married, with five children, before she's done shaking my hand."

Kit managed a small smile. "She's really a wonderful mother. I don't want you to think—"

"I don't," he reassured her. "She must be very happy with your father if she wants the same for you as badly as you seem to think. And for a while she can fantasize that I'll be the perfect husband. Will that be so terrible?"

Kit laughed, feeling more lighthearted and relaxed than she had in quite a few days. "I guess not." Her golden eyes twinkled teasingly at him. "I just hope she's up to it."

Stephen raised an eyebrow questioningly.

"You—as the perfect husband for me. That'll take a lot of fantasizing," she explained kindly, unable to restrain the impudent little grin that curled her lips.

"We've gotten very brave all of a sudden," he said suspiciously, turning the key in the ignition. "Why do I have the feeling I've just been very cleverly insulted?"

For a change, the traffic along the Golden State Highway was light, and Kit spent the time watching the familiar scenery flow by as Stephen's powerful Audi ate up the miles.

She also spent the time conjecturing about Stephen and how he had come to be such a strong advocate of marriage. Weren't most men just out for what they could get without having to pay the ultimate price of a wedding ring? Jeffery was a prime example of that. Of course, being married didn't preclude extramarital relationships—it certainly hadn't for Jeffery. But somehow she couldn't picture Stephen being so dishonest, despite his present aberration. Strangely Kit was very certain that once he said those vows, he would keep them.

So where did that leave her? Wildly attracted to a man engaged to another woman. What would her parents make of that, if she told them? Kit shuddered at the idea.

"Tell me who I'll be meeting," he suddenly asked, his deep voice jerking her from her uncomfortable thoughts, almost as though he had been reading her mind. "I don't think I want to be walking into this situation totally in the dark."

Kit's laughter was tinged with irony. "You should have thought about that before you suggested this crazy scheme." Then seeing the slight tightening of his mouth, she hurried to comply with his request. "You'll be meeting my parents, obviously. Elizabeth and Christopher Mallory."

He shot her a quick, teasing glance. "Tell me about him. Is he as accident-prone as his daughter?"

Kit's face softened lovingly. "No," she laughed, not at all offended by his provocation. "We're nothing alike. He's very calm and relaxed. Mellow, I guess, is the best word for him." She could sense Stephen's mirth and before he could say the words, admitted them herself. "As I said, I'm nothing like him. I guess he and my brother, Fredrik, have the most similar temperaments."

"Ah, yes. The matchmaking older brother. Will he be there?"

"Most definitely," Kit assured him. "He and Anne are sure to show up once they hear I'm bringing you along. Which means you'll also have the distinct privilege of meeting their two boys. Chris is nearly five and Beaner is almost four."

Stephen choked on a laugh, asking with raised brows, "Beaner?"

"Yes, well. Only Chris and I can call him that. His real name is Billy, but when he was two, he got into this sack of pinto beans and it made him horribly sick. He hasn't touched beans since."

"Hence, Beaner."

Kit nodded. "They're great kids," she enthused, her eyes sparkling a brilliant gold. "I absolutely adore them."

He studied her curiously, secretly fascinated that a woman who was so prickly about the institution of marriage, and treated the thought of motherhood so offhandedly, would find such obvious delight in their company. His eyes narrowed thoughtfully. "And their mother?" he asked. "What about her? What's she like?"

Kit answered him readily enough. "Anne was my best friend when we were kids."

"But no longer?" The question was casual, but Kit could hear the underlying interest in her response.

Her lips curved upward, her derisive glance letting him know she wasn't fooled for one second by his apparent nonchalance. "It's only natural that we'd go our separate ways as we got older," she reproved him lightly. "We're still friendly, even if we aren't as close as we once were."

"Hmm. All right, I'll grant you that," he yielded gracefully, "but you still haven't told me what she's like."

Kit tilted her head thoughtfully, considering how much she should reveal. "I don't know..." She hesitated deliberately, fully aware that she was piquing his interest. "Maybe I should let you discover that for yourself."

"A real couch potato, huh?" he guessed with a grimace. "And I suppose she's the reason you're not interested in marriage."

Kit's laughter was immediate and genuine. "I refuse to say more," she said with a chuckle, looking forward to his first glimpse of Anne. A more positive portraiture of wedded bliss he couldn't hope to find, unless, of course, it was her parents. But she'd let him discover that for himself. "You're in for an experience, and I certainly wouldn't want to spoil it for you!"

CHAPTER SIX

THE REST OF THE DRIVE was accomplished in record time, in a companionable silence broken only by Kit's quietly spoken directions. When they finally pulled up outside the Mallorys' large stucco house, Stephen glanced over at Kit, seeing the hint of anxiety creeping into her expressive gold eyes. "Is this where I take a deep breath, gird my loins, prepare to do battle and attempt to enter the lion's den?" he quipped lightly.

But before Kit could do more than smile her appreciation at his attempt to ease her apprehension, a pair of tiny whirlwinds burst through the front door of the house and rushed across the green expanse of lawn. "Aunt Kit! Aunt Kit!" they shrieked, flinging themselves against the side of the Audi.

"What are you two monsters doing here?" Kit demanded with a laugh, as she was practically dragged from the car by four rather sticky hands.

"We came to see you a'course," scoffed Chris, a black-haired, golden-eyed boy, larger than his younger brother by three full inches. "Soon as we heard you were gonna be here we begged and begged till Mom let us come over. She said she was just gonna give us to you. Do you want us?"

"Not on your life!" Kit cowered backward into the car in exaggerated alarm, her look of absolute horror drawing a spasm of giggles from the two boys.

"What did you bring us, Kit?" the youngest demanded greedily, rubbing a grubby hand across a freckle-splattered nose. Reddish-blond hair fell thickly across his brow, his soft blue eyes fastened hopefully on his aunt's smiling face.

"Shut up, Beaner," Chris whispered, nudging him with a sharp elbow. "You know you've got to wait till Mom isn't around to see."

Stephen's brows rose at that telling statement and bright rosy color swept across Kit's cheeks. "Yes, well..." Kit frowned fiercely at the pair, darting a swift glance at Stephen's faintly amused expression. "We'll discuss that later. I'm sure Grammy and Gramps are wondering where we are."

"Grammy said you were bringing home a man," Chris announced, studying Stephen with a critical eye. "Is this him?"

"Grammy said it was about time, too," Beaner piped up, not to be outdone by his big brother.

Kit groaned softly, her already reddened cheeks darkening further at Stephen's bark of laughter. "Why don't you two horrors disappear while I introduce Stephen to Grammy," she suggested pointedly, delighted when they took the hint and scampered off toward the back of the house. The fewer people around to witness this initial meeting the more comfortable she'd feel—especially a couple of big-eared little boys with even bigger mouths hanging on every word!

Elizabeth Mallory was a small woman, built very much like Kit, her figure still trim and athletic, her short, coppery hair lightly touched with gray. Her sparkling, golden-brown eyes, almost the mirror image of Kit's, lit up as they approached, and she hurried out to greet them, throwing her arms warmly around her daughter. "It's so good to see you," she cried, giving Kit an enthusiastic hug and kiss.

Kit gave her mother a tight squeeze. "It feels good to be home," she whispered in return. Then, suddenly remembering Stephen, she pulled away to make the introductions. "Mom, I'd like you to meet a friend, Stephen St. Clair." She carefully stressed the word friend, ignoring the caustic look Stephen shot her way.

Elizabeth smiled admiringly up at him. "Shall we make it Stephen and Elizabeth?" she suggested, her eyes twinkling merrily. "It's nice to finally meet you after all Kit's told us."

Stephen shot Kit a swift, penetrating look. "Please, don't believe a word she's said," he requested with a devastating grin. "Knowing your daughter, it probably was a most unflattering and totally inaccurate picture."

Elizabeth's eyes opened wide at that and she sent Kit an amused glance before blinking innocently up at Stephen. Kit closed her eyes with a wince, recognizing the expression and knowing that it didn't augur well for her. "Well," Elizabeth began, tongue firmly in cheek. "It wasn't all that terrible. Christopher assured me you couldn't be half as bad as she made out or Kit wouldn't be bringing you—"

"Mother!"

"Kit, I just want him to understand that your father and I fully intend to keep an open mind," Elizabeth explained artlessly. She turned back to Stephen. "Knowing Kit—" She hesitated delicately, and then shook her head in sorrow. "Well, when it comes to men, Kit does tend to be a rather poor judge—"

"Mother!"

"Well, darling, you do. Your father and I have commented on it many times. I just want your, er, 'friend' to know that we weren't really expecting the worst, despite your rather vivid description."

Stephen laughed. Taking Elizabeth's hand in his, he gave the older woman a conspiratorial wink, appreciating her sense of humor. "I think Kit's a little embarrassed about having a—" he broke off, smiling with a deliberate touch of boyish bashfulness "—well, having a man friend. Meeting the parents is always the hardest part."

"Oh, yes." Elizabeth Mallory sighed sympathetically, following Stephen's lead. She patted his arm with maternal understanding. "But the nice thing is that, years from now, when your children are bringing home their beaux for your approval, you two can sit back and laugh about it."

"We're planning five, you know," Stephen tossed in audaciously.

"*Stephen*, you promised—" Kit exploded, the rest of her furious words drowned out by the huge grandfather clock in the hallway chiming the noon hour. Its thunderous peal was instantly joined by half a dozen various mantel clocks all dutifully adding their own clamor to the din.

Elizabeth smiled serenely at Stephen's astonished expression, completely oblivious to her red-faced daughter's furious shouting. "It *is* something of a conversation stopper," she remarked with a laugh when the final stentorian bong had died away.

Kit opened her mouth in vehement protest, but could only force an indignant croak past her sorely abused throat. She was pointedly ignored.

"Christopher loves each and every one of his clocks," Elizabeth continued blithely. "So you can see why we couldn't part with a single one." She tucked a hand through Stephen's arm. "Come on, let me introduce you to my husband. You two can keep each other company while Kitten and I finish up with the preparations for lunch."

"Kitten?" Stephen mouthed silently to a visibly flushed Kit, his wide blue eyes bright with delight at the childhood nickname.

Kit stood stock-still watching the two disappear arm in arm toward the family room. Well! If that didn't take the cake, she didn't know what did!

"Kit," her mother's voice drifted back to her. "Are you coming or are you going to stand there all day?"

For a brief moment, Kit seriously contemplated standing there. In fact, it seemed the safest place for her. Then, gritting her teeth, she stopped by the family room to greet her father and, throwing a threatening scowl at a grinning Stephen, joined her mother in the kitchen.

"Not in the house for one minute and already I'm relegated to the kitchen like a proper little hausfrau," Kit grumbled under her breath.

"What did you say, dear?" Her mother looked up from the tray she was busy loading.

"Nothing!" Kit eyed her parent censoriously. "Just what was that little game you were playing out there? When I telephoned to ask if Stephen could come, I hardly said two words to you about him."

"Yes, I know that, dear—but he obviously didn't. For some strange reason, he seemed to think you'd given us a rather unfavorable opinion of him." She leveled a stern eye on Kit. "Why is that, do you suppose?" At Kit's garbled sputter, she inserted with expert precision, "You certainly found yourself a good-looking man, I must say—intelligent, good sense of humor and *single* to boot...."

Kit choked, catching the not-so-subtle dig at Jeffery. A faint note of desperation entered her voice when she'd finally gathered her wits sufficiently to speak. "We're really just friends," she insisted. "That's *all*."

Elizabeth looked up at her daughter, smiling serenely. "Yes, I know, dear. Stephen made that quite clear."

"But he didn't. He implied—"

"Yes, I know, dear. Kit, look for the mustard," her mother's muffled voice requested from the depths of the cupboard. "I can't seem to find it anywhere."

Kit gave up. It was obvious her mother was determined to put her own interpretation on things. And it was equally obvious that there wasn't a blessed thing she could do about it, except give in gracefully. Opening the refrigerator door, she took the mustard from the shelf, shaking her head. Typical. If it was right under her nose, her mother would never find it. It had to be hidden away in the farthest, most inaccessible corner for it to catch her eye.

"If you'd take the tray outside to the patio, Kit, I'll call everyone to lunch."

It was a beautiful, sunny California day, just perfect for an outdoor meal. The table was set for six, with two small folding trays placed off to one side for the boys. A platter of ham and roast beef covered in plastic wrap and a basket full of kaiser rolls had already been put out.

"Looks like mice have been at this meat," Kit commented loudly, unloading the tray. "There's some missing."

There was a loud rustling in the branches of a nearby tree and a dark head appeared, bright eyes gleaming mischievously. "Squeak! Squeak!"

"I heard that!" boomed a deep voice from directly behind her. "You two terrors come down from there and stay away from the food until lunchtime."

"Fredrik!" Kit spun around with a grin, hugging her large, copper-haired brother affectionately. "Where have you been hiding, you handsome lug?"

She was swept up into a massive bear hug. "I've been introducing myself to your, ah, to Stephen." He raised thick, shaggy brows, an irritated expression crossing his face. "Anne informed me that under no circumstances was I to ask you any questions about your, ah, about this Stephen guy," Fredrik complained. "Are things that serious between you two? Why is it I'm the last to know?"

"That's two questions," Kit snapped acidly, slipping free of his embrace. Then through gritted teeth, she stressed, "There is nothing *to* know! We are just friends!" She was beginning to sound like a broken record!

"Kit, my love, if you keep insisting that we're only friends, they'll really suspect something's up," Stephen commented dryly, as he appeared behind her. He threw a careless arm around her slender waist, pulling her firmly against him.

Kit inhaled sharply in stunned surprise. His taut muscles were pressed so closely to her soft curves that every single inch of him was indelibly impressed upon her tingling flesh. *I don't think I can handle this,* Kit thought nervously, squirming in an attempt to free herself, and realizing immediately that it was the wrong thing to do. The sensations that assailed her had her heart doing instant gymnastics, every inch of her skin sparking and exploding like a tiny firecracker. "Stephen..." she moaned softly in protest, painfully aware of her brother's fascinated attention.

Stephen tightened his hold, pressing a gentle finger to her lips to stop the threatened spill of words. "Now, now. No fighting in front of the relatives," he teased with a remonstrative shake of his head. He glanced toward Fredrik with a grin. "Prickly little thing, isn't she?"

It was too much. Kit simply couldn't resist. Without giving herself time to reconsider, she darted out her tongue and licked the fingers pressed so intimately to her parted lips. She could feel Stephen freeze against her and then she was swallowed up by his searing blue eyes. "I would have chosen a different method to silence you, if I'd known that would be your reaction," he growled into her ear and, helpless to stop herself, Kit dropped her gaze to his mouth, almost feeling the hard pressure of it against her unexpectedly dry lips. Oh, Lord, he was going to do it—right here in front of her entire family. He was going to kiss her—and if he didn't hurry up and do it soon, she knew *she'd* end up grabbing *him* and throwing him to the—

"It's a good thing Jesse isn't here to see this," a soft, musical voice remarked, breaking them apart. "His poor heart would be broken into a million pieces."

Held so tightly against him, Kit felt Stephen's sudden start of surprise as he turned to glance at the newcomer, the breath hissing from his lungs as though he'd just received an unexpected blow to his solar plexus.

"Your poor brother would be on the phone to one of his six-dozen girlfriends so fast, it would make your head spin," Kit snorted, her amusement at Stephen's reaction precisely what she needed to bring her overheated senses down from the danger level. Then, glancing from a speechless Stephen to an openly amused Anne, Kit chuckled. "It's a good thing you're happily married and that I'm not the jealous sort!" she greeted Anne affectionately. "Stephen." She nudged him in the ribs to gain his attention. "Meet your couch potato."

"Couch potato?" Anne mouthed questioningly at Kit with a gurgle of laughter. As a girl in high school, Anne had been lovely. Now as a fully matured woman, she was incredibly beautiful. Thick, ebony hair flowed in heavy waves past her shoulders, the dark locks framing a classically oval face. Silky black brows arched in perfect symmetry over soft, powder-blue eyes and delicate pink color dusted the pale creaminess of her high, elegant cheekbones.

She must have been as amused as Kit by Stephen's reaction, for her lips quivered, the soft curve of her mouth parting to reveal the gleam of perfect white teeth, and her beauty was instantly magnified by her radiant smile. She stepped forward in a graceful movement to offer her hand to Stephen. "We've been looking forward to meeting you this weekend," she murmured in a low, husky voice.

"I've been looking forward to it as well," Stephen replied instantly. "Kit told me about you, but somehow forgot to mention how lovely you are." The color in Anne's cheeks deepened as her teasing gaze met Kit's.

"But surely she wouldn't have gone so far as to call me a—a couch potato," Anne reproached him gently.

Dull color crept up under Stephen's tan and, to Kit's delight, he actually squirmed. "Oh, no! Of course not!" he said reassuringly. "She—I—"

"You would probably be able to answer her if you pulled your foot out of your mouth," Kit murmured, lowering her eyes to inspect her fingernails with an all-consuming fascination.

"Excuse us," Stephen muttered. A heavy hand landed on her shoulder and he yanked her off to one side, much to the intense interest of their audience. "Cute, Kit. Very cute," he growled furiously into her ear. "But let me assure you, you'll pay!"

"Oh?" she inquired airily, secure in the knowledge that he couldn't do a thing to her. Not with her family looking on. "And how do you plan to accomplish that?"

"Like this!" he snapped and proceeded to demonstrate with incredible expertise.

Instantly she was wrapped in his tight embrace, her head cushioned against the firmness of his shoulder, her face turned ruthlessly upward by the fingers gripping her chin. And then his mouth was on hers, his hard lips teaching her things she'd never known were possible. And all she could do was yield, too shocked to respond, too shaken to even protest. Not that she wanted to. In fact what she wanted, more than anything in the world, was to sink to the cool grass beneath them and give herself up to the ecstasy of his touch.

"Should we wait lunch, do you suppose?" Elizabeth's stage whisper acted like a douse of cold water.

Kit struggled free of Stephen's arms, turning to face the semicircle of spectators watching their performance. For a full minute, she prayed that the earth would open and swallow her whole.

"Boy, do you look funny, Kit!" giggled Beaner. "Your face is all red."

"That's 'cause he kissed her," Chris explained to his younger sibling in disdainful tones. "Mom does the same thing when Dad kisses her."

"Naw. Mom always kisses Dad back, real hard. Aren't you gonna kiss him back, Kit?"

Desperately Kit looked around for a way out of her predicament, her eyes falling on the table, which was all set for lunch. She cleared her throat noisily. "You've forgotten the mayonnaise, Mom. I'll just run in and get it."

Elizabeth sighed despairingly, her twinkling eyes letting Kit know she wasn't at all fooled by the attempted diversion. "I suppose it wouldn't be a Mallory meal if I hadn't forgotten something."

"Like the knives?" Fredrik asked helpfully, his determined footsteps following after his sister's.

Christopher Mallory peered over the top of his glasses. "Well, love. I hate to add my two cents, but I really think we'll need some cups if we want to have anything to drink." With that he joined the general exodus to the kitchen.

By the time everyone was finally seated, the conversation had become more general and lighthearted, only the peculiar glint in Stephen's eyes causing Kit any discomfort.

After a leisurely lunch, Fredrik and Anne announced they had other plans and had to leave. And it wasn't until Kit added her voice of persuasion to her parents' and the boys', that Chris and Beaner were permitted to remain behind.

"Come back and join us for dinner," Elizabeth urged them, reluctant to see the two leave so soon. "It's so rare to have the whole family together."

Fredrik's thick brows drew together in a scowl. "Who's cooking?" he asked bluntly, eyeing his mother with dark suspicion.

"Now, Fredrik." Elizabeth blinked up at him, the very picture of injured innocence. "I've tried this recipe before. I promise, nothing can go wrong this time."

Fredrik grimaced skeptically, giving his mother a quick peck on the cheek. "I'll believe that when I eat it. We'll be back by six."

"Well, Stephen, what do you say the two of us wander in and check out the exhibition football game that's on?" suggested Christopher, rising from the table and feeling in his pockets for his pipe. "You can tell me more about this company of yours. It's a profitable business, is it? Making toys?"

Stephen slanted a sardonic glance toward Kit, commenting blandly, "Actually, sir, it's people like your daughter who can make or break a company like mine. You'd be absolutely amazed at the difference just one individual can make."

"Is that so?" Christopher pursed his lips thoughtfully, leading the way back toward the house, not seeing the impudent tongue his daughter poked out at his guest. He paused in midstride. "By the way, my boy. You ever do any golfing?"

Kit chuckled. Little did Stephen know that he had just been successfully corralled for the afternoon. And in his own quiet, inoffensive way her father would learn everything there was to learn about Mr. Stephen St. Clair. Which left her free to get down to some very serious business. Like solid, uninterrupted playtime with her nephews.

MUCH LATER in the afternoon, feeling much more exhausted, Kit lay lazily on her back in the grass, Chris and Beaner on either side of her, gazing up at the sky. "I don't know, I think it looks a lot like a giant hornets' nest. See all the bees buzzing around it?"

"Naw," Beaner scoffed. "It's a great big hooty owl."

"You're both nuts. It's a popcorn popper that's blown its top," insisted Chris. He rolled over onto his stomach. "Hey, Kit, did you bring us something this time?"

She sat up, thrusting her hands into the pockets of her jeans. "Don't I always?" She pulled out two packets, each containing several different colored pellets. "Let's see here. We'll need a plate and some water. Let's see if we can raid the kitchen without Grammy catching us."

With that, they were up and off, Beaner successfully distracting his grandmother while Chris pinched a plate and Kit grabbed a glass of water. Racing out to the farthest corner of the yard, breathless with laughter, they huddled together over their prizes.

"Now watch," Kit instructed, dropping a black pellet onto the plate. She carefully poured a small amount of water over the strange black ball and almost instantly, to the boys' horrified fascination, it began to bubble and ooze, slowly expanding and stretching, first into a thick slime and then slowly taking shape and turning into a horribly bulbous black beetle.

Kit lifted it by one rubbery leg. "Repulsive, isn't it?"

"Yeah," breathed Chris reverently. "What do you call it?"

Kit frowned consideringly. "I haven't named this one yet. How about the Bugaboo Beetle? The red ones are the only ones we've really decided on—the Oozing Bloodsuckers. They turn into a hideous mass of wiggly worms."

The boys' eyes widened in delight. "Let's see that one!" they clamored.

Kit laughed at their bloodthirsty eagerness. "Not yet. Todd and I are going to alter the design so the pellets can go into water pistols. Then you can shoot them at each other and they peel right off without staining or anything. And the best part is they're—"

"Kit!"

"Whoops! That's Grammy. Come on, let's get this stuff cleaned up. We can try it again later. In the meantime I'm going to need your help naming these little guys. Besides the black beetle, we've got a yellow snake and a purple spider. What do you think? Can you come up with some suggestions for me?"

"Yeah!" the two chorused enthusiastically. "You help Grammy, we'll see what Gramps is doing. He'll give us some good names."

Gramps was found in the family room, puffing on his pipe in quiet conversation with Stephen—a conversation occasionally punctuated with vividly descriptive comments on certain mismanaged football plays. Chris and Beaner collapsed on the rug in front of the television.

"Well, how about Slithery for the snake?" Beaner offered. "Or Squiggly?"

"Squiggly could be a spider," Chris said. "Squiggly Spider and Slithery Snake. What do you think?"

"I can't think anymore. I'm too hungry," Beaner announced with a moan, his stomach growling noisily. He turned to his grandfather. "When's dinner, Gramps?"

A small cloud of fragrant pipe smoke drifted toward the ceiling. "I'm afraid I can't help you with that," Christopher replied impassively, fully aware of the dismay his comment engendered. "It's entirely up to Grammy tonight."

"Oh, no!" the two boys groaned in unison, exchanging horrified looks. "Not again!"

"Well, I smell something burning!" Chris announced in absolute disgust. "And if that's our dinner, I'm not eating it." Beaner nodded his head emphatically, in total agreement with his brother. There were no inducements great enough for that! Not even a trillion of Kit's surprise toys.

Stephen stirred in his chair, sniffing the air. "I think he's right, sir. It does smell like something's burning. Maybe we should offer to help."

Christopher inhaled deeply, testing the air for himself. "Yep. That's Elizabeth's pot roast all right. Very well done pot roast, true, but pot roast nonetheless." He continued to puff contentedly on his pipe, his attention on the football game.

Out of the corner of his eye Stephen caught Chris and Billy exchanging meaningful glances and frowned. "But perhaps if—" he began, only to be stopped by Christopher's faintly amused expression.

"I've been given my orders and it would be more than my life is worth to offer to help with this meal. You'll learn in time, Stephen, that when Elizabeth gets a notion in her head, that is that! Not even worth attempting to get her to see reason. And Elizabeth has this notion about who should cook for guests."

A suspicious little wisp of black drifted into the room. "Gramps, I see smoke," warned Beaner, eyeing the dark cloud with concern. "If you don't do something quick, you know what comes next." Chris nudged his brother and they snuggled together, burying their heads under their arms, their urgent whispers not quite audible to Stephen's attentive ears.

This was getting to be a bit much, Stephen thought, straightening in his seat in mild alarm. Just where the hell was Kit, anyway? He cleared his throat nervously. "Comes next?" he asked faintly.

"Yes, I know what comes next," Christopher reassured his youngest grandson absently, frowning at the television. "For crying out loud, when are they going to get referees who can see? That's the fourth miscall he's made this quarter."

"Perhaps if we turned the oven off or something," suggested Stephen, a hint of strain entering his voice as the dark wisps became slightly thicker, swirling around them in lazy little circles. "Elizabeth surely wouldn't object to that, would she?"

"Afraid she would, Stephen. *Holy mackerel!*"

Stephen shot to his feet. *"What?* What is it?" he panted, a distracted hand standing his hair on end.

"Did you see that interception? The quarterback practically handed the ball to him." Christopher shook his head in exasperation, struggling to peer through the dense cloud layer that now filled the room. He fanned his hands absently in the air. "Where do they get these guys, anyway?"

For a minute Stephen honestly thought his heart had stopped, and at the unexpected, earsplitting blare of the smoke detector going off, he nearly embedded his skull in the ceiling above him.

"There she blows!" howled Chris above the sound, clamping his hands over his ears.

"Oh, my God," Stephen mumbled in horror. "They're *all like her*! Why didn't I think of that?"

"Mother!" Kit's faint shriek could be heard over the deafening wail of the detector. "You promised you'd keep an eye on it this time! Turn the oven off, quick!" Harried feet raced back and forth as the hiss of water being turned to steam was broken intermittently by strange crackles and sizzles.

Christopher tapped his pipe ashes into an ashtray, sighing. "Chris, run and tell Kit to pull the battery out of that detector. Oh, and open the back door." He peered at the grinning boy over the top of his bifocals. "And Chris? Don't mention to Grammy that I told you to, right?" he suggested with a wink. "Billy, I think I hear someone at the front door. Be a good boy and get it, will you?"

He glanced up at Stephen, barely suppressed drollery in his dark eyes. "Sit down, my boy. Dinner won't be for a while yet. It'll take them some time to clear out all the smoke and burned food.''

''Never fear.'' Fredrik stepped into the room smiling brightly, a huge square box in his arms. ''We're back. Just in time, too, by the smell of things. I don't suppose anyone would care for pizza? It's an extralarge.''

CHAPTER SEVEN

THE CLOCKS striking midnight woke Kit. She yawned widely, conscious that having been away from home for so long had lessened her immunity to the noisy chiming. Rolling over in bed, she listened, a tiny smile softening her mouth. If the sounds of stealthy footsteps heading down the steps were anything to go by, Stephen was having as much trouble sleeping through all the clamor as she was. Kit flung back the covers and climbed out of bed. The least she could do was offer him some hot cocoa, she supposed, slipping on a wrap over her flimsy silk nightgown.

Padding down the steps and through the silent house, Kit pushed open the kitchen door to reveal a very weary Stephen. He sat slumped at the kitchen table, his heavily shadowed eyes half closed, his fair hair attractively tousled.

A warmly sympathetic smile tugged at the corners of Kit's mouth. "Believe it or not, you do get used to the noise. After a while, you don't hear it anymore," she murmured lightly, stepping into the room. "It just takes time."

"Not in a thousand years," groaned Stephen.

"How about some hot cocoa?" Kit offered. "It might help." She searched through the bottom cabinets, finally pulling out a saucepan.

He eyed her suspiciously. "You didn't learn how to make it from your mother, did you?" he asked with the merest hint of alarm.

Kit smothered a laugh, struggling to keep her tone squelchingly severe. "Don't make fun of my mother."

"I wasn't," he hastened to reassure her. "At least, it wasn't meant unkindly." He scratched at his whisker-roughened chin. "It has shown me one thing I've been very curious about." At the questioning glance she shot him, he elaborated teasingly, "Where you get some of your more interesting traits. You were right—you're not like your father."

"Very funny!" The saucepan hit the stove top with a little bang and Kit opened the refrigerator to pull out a carton of milk. Her voice sharpened noticeably as she said, "My mother may not be the world's greatest cook, I'll grant you that, considering it's my dad who usually takes care of the meals. Unfortunately, Mom has this need to prove herself when people first come to visit. She feels she has to play out the role of being the stereotypical housewife."

"Which means cooking the dinner."

Kit turned to face him, quick to defend her parents. "Yes. But that doesn't mean she's less of a mother, just because she can't cook. In my book, she's pretty darn terrific. They both are."

Stephen studied her aggressive stance and smiled disarmingly. "I agree. From the look of things, they've managed to work out a very successful arrangement. These days, that's not too common."

"They've always been like that," Kit said with a shrug. "They give and take."

His eyes watched her, a strange, almost confused expression in their dark blue depths. "Explain it to me, Kit. Why, with examples like your parents, and Anne and Fredrik, are you so determined to stick to a career? Do you really believe it will bring you more satisfaction than the love of a man, or the joy of motherhood?"

Kit didn't answer immediately, instead turning toward the stove to switch on the gas flame beneath the saucepan of milk. Then, her expression thoughtful, she joined him at the table. "Maybe I gave you the wrong impression at dinner the other night, Stephen," she began, choosing her words carefully. "I really don't have any objection to marriage and children. In fact, I can only hope that some-day I'll be as fortunate in my choice as the rest of my family has been."

"That doesn't answer my question," he interrupted.

Kit sighed, her gold eyes unusually serious. "I think, in a way, it does. You seem to believe I have to make a choice, an either/or deal. But there's nothing wrong with what I want. Why can't I have it all?" she asked reasonably. "It's not so unusual these days for a woman to combine raising a family with having a career."

Stephen took a moment to absorb her words. "Was that a secret ambition of your mother's?" he finally asked, his tone revealing his frustration as he tried to fit the pieces together in a way that made sense to him. "Did she want to work and couldn't?"

Kit shook her head with a defeated little laugh. "Stephen, you're looking for something that just isn't there. It—it's as if you're trying to uncover some deep, dark secret that's driving me to this decision. But there isn't any. My mother was very traditional in her outlook. She stayed home and took care of the two of us while Dad worked, because that's what she wanted to do. Can you really see my father ordering her to the kitchen, if where she wanted to be was out in the workplace?"

"Then why—?"

She reached out and took his hand in hers. "Because I love my job. Because I love doing something positive and creative with my life. Because I haven't met anyone I wish to marry." She ruthlessly thrust down the little voice that called her a liar. "And because I don't have any children to worry about."

"And when you do?"

Kit shrugged easily. "I guess I'll worry about that when it happens."

"That's a cop-out!"

"Why?" she demanded, her fingers tensing against his. "It's no more of a cop-out than your unilaterally deciding that a woman can't do it all. Let's turn the tables. What's your deep, dark secret? How did you get your warped ideas about career women?"

"My attitude toward career women is not warped," he coolly denied, his jaw squaring decisively.

Kit threw him a skeptical look. "You wouldn't marry one, would you?"

Stephen remained silent for a moment, his face drawn in remote and uncompromising lines. "No," he finally admitted, a little tightly, pulling his hand away from hers. He stood up, his movements unusually restless as he started searching through the cupboards for some coffee cups.

"Try the corner cabinet," Kit suggested impatiently, her narrowed gaze willing him to continue. "So—"

He set the thick mugs on the table and shoved his hands into the pockets of the black robe that covered his blue silk pajamas, a faintly bitter expression darkening his eyes. "You were lucky, Kit, whether you fully realize it or not. You had a mother at home to care for you when you'd scraped a knee, or bruised an elbow. Someone to give you her time, listen to your little stories, to read to you, maybe to join in your games. I didn't."

"But—" Kit began, thinking of Victoria St. Clair.

Stephen's laugh was harsh, able to read her thoughts with ease. "You've met my mother. Can you imagine the president of Clairington Cosmetics permitting a grubby little boy or girl to crawl up onto her impeccably groomed lap and muss her perfect hair or makeup? Her career and image always came first, always. It meant everything to her." His voice dropped to a bitter murmur. "Even more than her children."

Kit stared at him in horrified disbelief. Of course! Why hadn't she realized? How could she have been so stupid not to recognize those compelling features—she must have seen Victoria St. Clair's face countless times before. How could anyone help but know her? She had been emblazoned on magazine covers for over two decades.

Victoria St. Clair was the ultimate example of the American dream come true, her meteoric rise to fame and fortune nothing short of miraculous. What had started as a tiny, neighborhood beauty salon operated from a run-down garage, had in the space of a few, short years become an international cosmetics conglomerate. No wonder Stephen felt the way he did. Running such an empire wouldn't have left Victoria St. Clair much time or energy for anything else, especially not the demands of small—

Kit's eyes widened. "You said children, plural, a grubby little boy—and girl? You have a sister? You've never mentioned any siblings."

If anything Stephen's face became even more remote, his expression letting Kit know that she was trespassing. "Had," he bit out. "I had a sister. She's—she died, many years ago."

"Stephen, I'm so sorry!" Kit whispered. "No wonder you acted so strangely at the restaurant when I told you about Fredrik—"

But before she could say anything more, he interrupted her, deliberately attempting to put her on the defensive. "So tell me—is that what you want for your children? To put them in second or third or fourth place, depending on how you're feeling at the moment?"

"No!" Kit exclaimed, certain that she'd never, ever do such a thing. "Stephen, you can't cast everyone in the same mold as your mother! It must have been very difficult for her to balance the responsibilities of her position at Clairington with those of her family."

"You're defending her?" Stephen demanded incredulously. Then his features hardened, settling into cynical lines, his mouth curling bitterly. "But of course. How foolish of me to try to explain to a diehard career woman the bewilderment and hurt of children whose mother has abandoned them in favor of the glamour and excitement of her job."

"That's not fair!" Kit returned vehemently. "I only meant—"

"Kit, the milk." Kit stared at him blankly for an instant before hurrying over to the stove. She wasn't attempting to justify Victoria's neglect of her children, was she? Surely she wasn't so unfeeling, so insensitive. Images of her own childhood began to rise before her—a childhood that must have been very different from Stephen's.

She and Fredrik picnicking with her parents on warm Sunday afternoons. Her mother taking them to the park or walking them to the library. Fredrik's swimming lessons. Her school plays. A smile softened her mouth as pictures flooded her mind, pictures of burned cookies and numerous other culinary disasters as well as a multitude of other small things her mother had attempted to do for her children throughout their childhood.

Motherhood had been Elizabeth Mallory's career, and if she had ever felt dissatisfied with it, she'd never once let on. Kit's expression sobered when she compared it to what Stephen and his sister must have experienced as children. She could understand why he felt the need for a traditional wife, considering what she'd just learned, but that still didn't mean he was right.

She poured the hot milk into the mugs, adding a heaping spoonful of cocoa to each, the spoon clinking furiously against the sides. "So career women are taboo because of your mother," Kit stated in as even a voice as she could manage, not quite sure why it was suddenly such an effort to act and speak normally.

"That's it in a nutshell," he agreed harshly. "My mother is proof positive that you can't do it all. So the woman I choose for my wife will feel the exact same way I do about marriage and children—and a career."

"You mean *lack of* a career, don't you?" Kit retorted acidly. "I mean, that is what we're discussing here. Imposing your prejudices on some poor woman, forcing her to give up her life, her job. Forcing her to give up everything, and for what? Just to be your—" She broke off, the words sticking in her throat. To be your wife.

Oh, God, Kit thought in numbed dismay. To be his wife. To live with this man, be loved by him, share intimacies with him. She couldn't bear to think about it. For the mere thought of being part of such an existence brought a merciless pain that threatened to tear her apart. It was a life that could never be hers. Their stances were so distant, so diametrically opposed that she could see absolutely no room for compromise. That fact had just been brought home to her.

And why should it matter so much? Why should the knowledge that there could never be any possibility of a relationship with Stephen cause her such anguish? Kit bit her lip, wanting to protect herself from the wave of despair that threatened to drown her, and couldn't. It wouldn't matter so much—if she didn't love him. And that was one fact she couldn't hide from any longer.

She loved Stephen. For all his crazy ideas about women and careers, for all his stubbornness and pride, for all that and, perhaps, because of it, she loved him.

"Yes, she'd have to give up all thought of a career to be my wife," Stephen finished her aborted sentence in calm tones, inclining his head in arrogant agreement. "Sorry if you find the prospect so unappealing," he added dryly, taking the steaming cup she proffered before resuming his seat at the table.

For a minute, Kit wanted to laugh hysterically. Unappealing? If only it were. If only the prospect weren't so horribly, intensely appealing. Kit sank onto her chair, Stephen's cool eyes unexpectedly spearing her. "That explains me. Now for your side. Are you sure there isn't anything that's helped feed your obsession with a career, somewhere along the way?"

"What are you talking about?" Kit stirred uncomfortably beneath the steely directness of his gaze. "I've explained that there's no particular reason why I prefer to commit myself to a career."

Stephen took a swallow of the warm cocoa and raised an eyebrow derisively. "You're absolutely certain Jeffery had nothing to do with this determination of yours?"

Kit's eyes widened and then filled with sudden anger. "Who told you about him?"

"Why? So you can take your hot little temper out on them?" Stephen shook his head grimly. "Oh, no, sweetheart. I'm not letting you sidetrack the issue that way." He leaned across the table toward her. "Tell me, Kit. Are you sure all this hasn't something to do with your aborted love affair with Jeffery—jilted by your lover, you turn to work for solace?"

Kit gave him a furious look. "For your information," she bit out, "I wasn't jilted. Some unpleasant realities came to light and I dumped him."

"Right." Stephen inclined his head sardonically. "Let me guess, *he* wanted a traditional sort of wife, too."

"No. He already had a traditional sort of wife. He wanted a traditional sort of mistress." The startled intake of his breath gave Kit a small measure of satisfaction. "Naturally, I declined."

"I'm sorry Kit, I didn't realize," Stephen murmured sympathetically, the sudden warmth in his eyes oddly protective. "But even so, considering how hurt you must have been, it's all the more understandable that you'd turn to your—"

"No!" Kit turned determinedly away from his compelling blue eyes. It offered too much temptation. Temptation she couldn't afford to give in to. "I was hurt, true, but when you're not really in love with a man to begin with, you quickly discover that the hurt isn't so much to your heart as it is to your pride."

"Ah—the ultimate defense," he murmured softly, a wealth of understanding in the low, husky voice. "And painfully familiar."

"It's not a defense," Kit insisted, her chair scraping back across the floor. She stood up and moved away, wrapping her arms about her waist, unaware of how revealing her stance was. "It was a long time ago—"

"While you were still in college, perhaps?" Stephen suggested, observing with interest her wary agreement. "And at a rather vulnerable period in your life, too, hmm?"

"No—" Kit replied, shaking her head firmly.

Stephen stood, his broad frame assuming nerve-rackingly huge dimensions. "A first love affair," he guessed shrewdly, taking a step toward her, knowing he blocked any further retreat. "A young woman just starting out in life, forming initial impressions on love—and finding it doesn't quite live up to her expectations."

Frantically Kit continued to shake her head.

Stephen took a step closer, tilting his head to one side, questioningly. "And since love didn't work out, perhaps you decided to concentrate on a career instead."

"You're mistaken," Kit insisted tightly.

"Am I? I don't think so." Stephen reached for her, his powerful arms closing around her, drawing her into his warm embrace. "Let me show you how good it can feel to be a woman. To know the love and care of a man. Can any job give you this?'' Then his face came down, blotting out everything, and his lips consumed hers.

For an instant, Kit resisted, remaining stiff in his arms. But it was only for an instant. She wanted Stephen's touch too much to fight him for long and, with a sigh, Kit relaxed, her body becoming pliant in his embrace. Mindlessly she reached for him, her fingers sliding into his hair, her body arching against his broad chest. Her mouth parted beneath his, opening for him, reveling in his gentle ministrations. Just this once, she'd allow herself to experience again the ecstasy he could so easily arouse in her. Just this one last time.

"Stephen, please," she whispered, her voice catching raggedly in her throat as she pressed herself against his hard masculinity, seeking the security of his strength. "This isn't going to solve anything. We can't even agree on the basics, let alone . . .'' Her voice trailed off miserably.

"I don't know about that. We seem in complete agreement about one thing," he told her tenderly, his hands stroking her shoulders. "Have you any idea what you do to my equilibrium, Kit? Even while you're driving me up the wall with your hardheadedness, that sweet mouth of yours tempts me, challenges me to explore its softness.'' His hand moved to her chin, tilting it upward, his darkened blue gaze blazing down into the golden pools of her eyes.

Kit shook her head in painful denial. "How can you say that when I'm everything you despise most—'' His lips stopped her words, his tongue caressing the honeyed warmth of her mouth.

"No," he whispered against her, reassuring her. "Never that. Don't think about it, not now. Just feel—feel what it can be like for us.'' He pulled her closer, his intense ardor easily transmitted through the thin material of their nightclothes. His mouth hardened over hers, his touch sweeping her to heights she'd never before imagined, fan-

ning scorching flames of desire. She shuddered against
him.

"Kit, I have to touch you, feel the silk of your skin."
Gently he pushed the thin wrap from her shoulders, and
after a slight hesitation, Kit helped him, her need out-
weighing every other thought and consideration. With
fingers that trembled, she freed her arms from the con-
stricting confines of her robe, and it drifted freely to her
waist, held only by its loosely knotted belt.

Kit's breath caught in her throat and her heart pounded
frantically as Stephen's hand slid from her shoulders to
lightly cup her breasts, stroking the heated skin through
the nearly transparent silk of her nightgown. Her head fell
backward, exposing the creamy length of her neck, and
obediently, Stephen's mouth traced delicately downward,
finding the sensitive area beneath her ear, and then lower
still, his mouth nudging the narrow straps of her nightgown to one side, revealing the full, pale curves of her
breasts.

"Kit," he groaned harshly, his breath hot against the
side of her neck. "I want you, sweetheart." His hands
moved skillfully over her, intent on finding ways to give
her the most pleasure, encouraged and excited by the
helpless cries that escaped from her throat.

"Please," Kit begged mindlessly, gasping when he suddenly slid an arm beneath her knees and swept her up into
his strong arms. She tightened her arms around his neck,
her eyelids falling shut, her lips nuzzling the raspy skin
beneath his jaw.

"Kit!" he suddenly muttered.

"Oh, yes, Stephen," Kit whispered back passionately,
straining against him, her lips moving easily across the taut
muscles of his face, responding ardently to the sudden ur-
gency in his voice.

"Kit!" Reluctantly she opened her eyes, puzzled at the
sudden tensing of his body.

Then she heard someone clear his throat, and swung her head around toward the kitchen door.

And there, framed in the doorway, taking in the situation in one long, all-encompassing look, stood Christopher and Elizabeth Mallory.

"Um—I don't suppose you'd care for some coffee first?" Elizabeth suggested weakly.

"OF ALL THE THINGS you could have said, did you have to tell them *that*?" Kit demanded furiously, frantically pacing the floor, unable to stand the constrained silence between them for another second.

She cringed at the unexpected crash that came from the small kitchen of her duplex, then eyed Stephen warily when his rumpled head poked through the door. "Just what the hell did you want me to tell them?" he snarled back, waving the jagged remains of a glass at her. "The circumstances were pretty damning! Where do you keep your broom and dustpan, anyway?"

"In the pantry—the same place most people keep it! Well, you could have come up with something better than that," she insisted over the sounds of his energetic sweeping. "This can't be the first time you've been caught in a tight corner with a woman and had to do some fast-talking to get yourself out." She regretted the nasty crack the minute she'd said it.

Instantly Stephen appeared from the kitchen, dark red color flooding his lean cheeks, a convulsive movement jerking the muscles in his jaw. "The conversation sort of dried up on me," he finally managed to growl savagely, his fists clenching and unclenching in an ominous manner. "I mean, there wasn't a hell of a lot I could say to them at midnight while holding their sweet, innocent, half-undressed little girl in my arms."

Kit was not mollified. "Well, the next time you get the urge to play Rhett Butler, do me a favor. Suppress it!"

"No problem, Scarlett!" he shot back at her. "Believe me, that's the last time I'll let vulnerable golden eyes and a sweet welcoming mouth seduce me to the point of forgetting where I am!"

Kit blinked at him, the anger draining from her at his unexpected words. "Is that what happened, Stephen?" she asked softly, searching his shuttered face for some indication of his true feelings. "Did you really forget where we were?"

"Yes."

Kit hid a smile. His response had been brusque to the point of rudeness and held more than a little resentment, but the admission filled her with a secret elation. "But to tell them we're engaged," she sighed, pressing a weary hand to her brow. "You're already engaged. You can't be engaged to two people at the same time."

Stephen stared at her as though she'd grown a second head. "What the hell are you talking about now?"

"Your—other—fiancée," Kit enunciated very carefully, her eyes flashing with renewed resentment. "Remember?"

"My other fiancée," he repeated faintly. "Offhand, I have to admit, I don't remember her. Perhaps you'd be so kind as to clue me in?"

"Very funny, Stephen," Kit snapped indignantly. "Your sense of humor has me rolling in the aisles. But the joke's over now. I'm serious! You've got to do something about this situation."

"Gladly. I don't suppose you happen to know her name or—" he quirked a roguish eyebrow upward inquiringly "—where I might find this poor, much-maligned person? After all, if I'm to end things, it would help to know where to look for her."

"If I were Lydia, I think I'd kill you for that," Kit said angrily, not appreciating his levity in the least. "How could you be so cavalier? If she ever heard about this weekend, she'd be furious. And I wouldn't blame her one bit.''

Stephen froze, understanding suddenly dawning. His lids flicked swiftly downward to conceal the gleam of unholy amusement that lit his eyes. ''Ah, yes. Poor, dear Lydia.''

Kit began to pace back and forth in front of him. ''I just don't understand! How could you do it? I mean, I know there's a certain amount of chemistry between us.''

Stephen clicked his tongue in admonishment.

''Okay, maybe a *lot* of chemistry.'' The words were wrung reluctantly from her. ''And, to be perfectly honest, I haven't exactly offered much resistance— Stop that!'' she burst out, infuriated by the sanctimonious expression he had assumed. ''You can look as piously angelic as you want, but it still doesn't excuse your behavior! How could you kiss me—''

''Easily, my sweet,'' he assured her innocently. ''I just do this.'' And he proceeded to demonstrate in a very, very effective manner.

Kit tore herself out of his arms. ''Cut that out! That's precisely what I'm talking about. You can't keep kissing me when you're going to marry Lydia.''

''And who says I'm going to marry Lydia?'' Stephen asked ever so gently, something in his voice making Kit unaccountably wary.

''*You* did.'' She glared at him with a mixture of defiance and confusion. ''Or she did. I don't remember! Everyone says it. I heard her myself, in your office, discussing wedding plans with you. And don't try to tell me that rock on Lydia's finger came out of a gum machine—''

''St. Clair, Kit. Lydia St. Clair.''

''Because I won't believe it. It's common knowledge about the two of you, you know. The whole office, everyone, they all say—'' His calmly spoken words finally penetrated her brain, bringing her up short. "Lydia ... St. Clair?" Her voice rose to a squeak. "You've already married her? All this time, while you've—while we've—you've been married? You—you *rat*!"

"Has anyone ever told you that you have a screw loose?" Stephen asked lightly, almost kindly, before giving full rein to his temper. "She's my *cousin*, you brainless twit—my *only* cousin! My father's brother's daughter, if you need to know the precise connection. If you'd asked me about her in the first place, I would have told you that." All six-plus feet of bristling male aggression moved to stand over Kit's shrinking, wide-eyed form. "And, by the way, thank you so very much for assuming I'd be such a heel as to make love to you while engaged to another woman. That makes me feel just great!"

"You're not engaged?" Kit said, a broad, foolish grin spreading across her face.

"Of course I'm not. I'm no Jeffery," he snapped, highly affronted. "How could you even think it? And now look at the mess we're in because of you."

"Don't blame me. This is all your fault," she informed him tartly, wild excitement surging through her veins. He wasn't engaged. *He wasn't engaged*! "I warned you the whole thing would be a disaster. But did you listen to me? Oh, no!"

Stephen grunted in wry amusement. "You're right. I should have listened." He collapsed wearily onto the couch, his gaze rising to mock her. "It's totally my fault. I should have realized that your entire family would be as crackers as you are."

"They are not. I am not!"

Stephen ignored her brief explosion. Exhausted, he closed his eyes and rubbed a hand across his jaw, then spoke reflectively. "I'll have you know that I led a fairly normal, uncomplicated life until you blew into it. I had everything carefully planned. Start my own company—a rather exciting and innovative company at that." His lids struggled upward a millimeter and he shot her an accusing glance. "Or it was. Find a nice, traditional sort of woman to fall in love with, get married, have children. It was all very carefully mapped out. I don't remember one Kit Mallory being included. No, in fact I'm absolutely positive no one by that name was in there. And now all my plans are totally shot to hell!"

Kit stared at him, a flash of anger bringing a bright gold spark to her eyes. She shook her head pityingly. "Poor thing. You've been without sleep for too long. You're obviously delirious."

"I probably am," he instantly agreed, a huge yawn catching him by surprise. "I haven't caught a wink for over thirty-six hours now. I think that gives me the right to be slightly delirious."

Kit hesitated for a moment, her concern suddenly sincere. He did look worn-out. "Stephen, it's late. Why don't you go home to bed."

There was no ignoring the suggestive gleam in his eye. "Why don't I just bed down right here? That way, you could join me," he murmured huskily, stretching his long body out on the couch. "Of course, I can't promise we'll get all that much rest."

"I thought you were delirious with exhaustion." Kit couldn't resist the taunt.

"Never that delirious, nor that exhausted," came the instant retort. And then his lids slid closed and he was asleep.

KIT PROWLED restlessly around the kitchen, picking up her coffee cup and frowning at the dark dregs swirling around the bottom, before setting it down again. *Relax,* she scolded herself. He'll be awake soon, and then, once he's gone, you can go to bed and get some much-needed sleep. She paced to the doorway between the kitchen and the living room for the hundredth time, not realizing how hungrily her eyes rested on the dark shape occupying her couch.

Unable to resist the urge any longer, Kit slipped into the room and stood at the foot of the sofa, staring down at Stephen. He lay on his back, his head turned to one side, his breathing deep and regular. Her eyes darkened with emotion, lingering lovingly on his rumpled head and the thick, blond hair that curled freely around the sharp angles of his face. So much for the cool and aloof executive, Kit thought with a tiny, wistful smile. In repose, with his features softened and so oddly vulnerable, he looked more like an overgrown schoolboy than the president of his own company.

Is this what a son of his would look like? Kit wondered with a sudden bittersweet yearning. Would his child have that glittering head of hair, those long golden lashes? In her mind's eye she could almost see the boy, each year becoming more and more like Stephen as his childlike body grew and developed, as his features were honed and chiseled into his father's image. *Stephen's child, his son.* She struggled to catch her breath against the pain that thought caused her.

"I was dreaming about you." The quiet, sleepy voice took Kit by complete surprise and sent her eyes flying to meet Stephen's tender gaze. "And when I woke up, there you were, looking at me." His voice dropped to a deep, husky whisper. "Your expression—it was so strange, Kit, almost . . . sad. What were you thinking about?"

Kit stood before him, helplessly mute. Unable to respond. Afraid to respond.

As though understanding what she couldn't bring herself to say aloud, Stephen reached for her hand, pulling her down toward him until she, too, was stretched out on the couch, her body wedged tightly into the protective curve of his. "It'll be okay, Kit. Don't worry." His mouth brushed the top of her head. "We'll work it out. We'll work it all out somehow."

Swallowing convulsively, Kit turned her head into the crook of his shoulder, hiding the hot tears that filled her eyes.

CHAPTER EIGHT

'CAN YOU BELIEVE this rain?''

"No," Kit sighed, leaning back against the sturdy wall of Stephen's chest, her somber eyes on the steady downpour outside the office window. "It always takes me by surprise. You get so used to blue skies and gentle breezes that you forget that it's nearly autumn already," Kit murmured. "I guess that's what Southern California does to you. It lulls you into thinking that the sun will shine every day and then—bam." She shivered dramatically. "Reality hits you like a wet blanket."

"Don't, Kit." She could feel the tension tautening Stephen's body and felt a small pang of regret at being the cause. "I thought we agreed to let things run their natural course for a while. It hasn't been all that long yet, only a little over a month since we visited your parents."

Exactly five weeks and six days, Kit thought with a melancholy smile, and she'd rejoiced in every moment of that time they'd had together, refusing to think about it ever ending. Until now. She turned around, burying her face against the scratchy wool of Stephen's blue sweater, wrapping her arms tightly around his waist. "How can you read me so easily?" came her muffled complaint. "All I said was that—"

"Was that there comes a time when you have to face facts," he cut in ruefully, though Kit could hear an almost fierce undertone to his words. "Well, I'm not ready to do that yet. I want to hold on to my summer sunshine for a little longer, before I have to start worrying about snow and ice and dreary days.''

"It doesn't snow down here, and you know it.'' Kit scoffed, poking him playfully in the ribs, hoping to tease him into a better frame of mind. "And the only ice you'll ever have to worry about are the cubes they put in your Perrier.''

"Pragmatist!'' Stephen looked down at her tenderly, the strain easing from his features, a loving gleam brightening his eyes. "I like it when you wear your hair loose like this,'' he told her quietly, running his hands through the long, honey-colored strands. "It's like bronze and gold silk all mixed up together. Much better than that braid.''

Kit felt the heat rising in her cheeks. "You know why I usually tie it back.''

Stephen's mouth quirked at the memory, his long-fingered hands gently cupping her upturned face. "I vaguely recall your mentioning something about that.'' His eyes twinkled down into hers. And then the smile faded away, to be swiftly replaced by a more ardent expression. Slowly he lowered his head, capturing her lips with his, nibbling their soft fullness. "Come upstairs with me, Kit. Now. This minute,'' he breathed hungrily against her mouth. "I'll draw the drapes so we won't know whether it's sunny or rainy or hailing golf balls. We could spend tonight and all day Sunday in bed. Alone. Together. Making love until nothing in the world exists anymore except you and me.''

"You make it sound so wonderfully tempting,'' Kit whispered unevenly, sliding her hands lightly over his and tilting her head back away from the warmth of his touch. "But your mother's party—''

He pressed a finger to her lips, stopping her words. "Shh. You don't have to make any excuses. I told you before, I'll wait until you're ready.'' He dropped a quick, affectionate kiss on the tip of her nose, changing the subject. "You aren't nervous about tonight, are you?"

Kit struggled to keep her expression from revealing her thoughts, knowing it was a wasted effort. Stephen was much too astute. "A little," she finally admitted. "Your mother's not stupid. We both knew it was only a matter of time before she found out about us."

"Maybe it had something to do with our showing up at Lydia's wedding together," Stephen suggested dryly.

"Mmm." Kit shrugged, slanting him a teasing glance from beneath dark lashes. "More likely it had something to do with the way you *kissed* me at Lydia's wedding! Although I doubt Lydia noticed. She didn't seem aware of anything except Peter that day. But your mother sure did."

And yet, surprisingly, Victoria St. Clair hadn't seemed to mind, Kit mused, with something akin to shock. In fact, Kit had the distinct impression that she'd been secretly pleased by the knowledge. Not that Victoria, as she'd insisted Kit call her, had actually said so. If anything, she was more sharp-tongued than ever. It was just something in those beautiful, dark eyes—relief?—that had given Kit the impression that she'd approved the relationship.

"Anyway, I'm looking forward to seeing this new place she's bought. I don't think I've ever been to a housewarming before," Kit said on a more positive note. "Are there going to be hordes of people there, do you think?"

Stephen grimaced. "Probably, knowing my mother. But then that'll make it easier for us to make an early escape and find something more—" his mouth curved suggestively "—enjoyable to do. Mother's parties tend to be a bit too sophisticated for my palate. Let me get the address and then we'd better push off. You ready?"

It took them half an hour to find the address Victoria St. Clair had given Stephen. And when they finally pulled up outside the tiny house tucked snugly beneath a stand of towering pines, Stephen made no move to leave the car, first frowning down at the slip of paper in his hand, and then peering through the heavy rain at the number on the side of the house. "This can't be it," he muttered.

"It *is* rather—small," Kit hesitantly agreed.

"That's putting it mildly. The entire thing could fit into the living room of her last place. I must have gotten the number wrong."

Just then the front door opened, a welcoming glow of warm light spilling out onto the porch. "That's Mother," Stephen said as a figure waved energetically at them from the doorway. "This must be it, after all." He quirked an eyebrow upward in amusement. "Well, it should prove interesting to see what she's up to this time."

Victoria's new house was the complete opposite of what Kit had expected. Instead of the anticipated mansion with an elaborate chrome-and-glass interior, she found an extremely attractive, comfortably designed home.

"Surprised you, didn't I?" Victoria demanded of Stephen the moment they'd stepped inside. "Well, I've got news for you. This isn't my only surprise of the evening." And with that cryptic comment, she swept them along on a tour of the house. "It's really larger than it looks from the outside. Two bedrooms, two-plus baths, living room, dining room, a cozy little family room and the most modern kitchen imaginable." She shot a flippant glance at Stephen, adding dryly, "I guess I'll have to take some cooking lessons so I can use it."

Kit was impressed by the beauty and charm of the place. Each room seemed to flow into the next, and the furniture had been chosen for comfort rather than fashion or style. And yet there was a special flare, an unusual combination of texture, light and color that enchanted and stimulated the senses while at the same time managing to soothe and please the eye.

"It's a beautiful home, Mother, very unusual," Stephen complimented Victoria sincerely when she finally led them back to the family room. He settled into a love seat in front of a crackling fire, pulling Kit down beside him. "Did you design it yourself? It's quite different from your place in L.A."

"Yes, it's all my very own creation," Victoria said, laughing in delight, the sound rich and husky. "No one else would dare take the blame. The designer I worked with thought I was quite mad. When I insisted on cementing the stones I'd gathered from the beach to the wall of the spare bedroom, he was sure of it. But the final straw, as far as he was concerned, was the waterfall and flower garden I wanted to go in there with it! He called me several unrepeatable names, and walked out. Oops. There's the doorbell. I'll be right back." And with an air of nervous excitement, she hurried from the room.

Kit glanced at Stephen, surprised to see a pensive look on his face. "She's changed," Kit offered tentatively. "She seems—I don't know—freer, happier."

"Something's up," Stephen stated grimly. "And I'm not sure I'm going to like hearing what it is."

When Victoria returned, it was with Lydia and a serious, dark-haired young man in tow, whom Kit vaguely remembered as the nervous bridegroom.

"You've all met before," Victoria announced breezily, "though considering the occasion, I'll refresh your memories. Lydia and Peter Vallance, Kit Mallory. And of course you know Stephen."

"I'll assume from that introduction that you were at the wedding, but I don't—" Lydia shook her head, offering Kit a shy, apologetic smile. "I'm sure we've met even before then—Stephen's office, wasn't it? Though, considering my state of mind at the time, I must have left a very poor impression." At Victoria's questioning look, Lydia blushed painfully, guilty eyes flying to Stephen for assistance.

"I'm sure it was just premarital jitters," Kit put in swiftly, suddenly remembering the reason for Lydia's visit—to complain about Victoria's interference with the wedding plans. It was obvious to Kit that the younger woman didn't want her aunt to know anything about the conversation, and so she asked lightly, "Did Stephen tell you who I thought you were?" and proceeded to relate in hilarious detail her confusion over Lydia's identity.

By the time she was finished, the awkward moment had been smoothed over, and Lydia threw Kit a warm, grateful look. "I thought you invited us to a party," Stephen questioned his mother. "Are we early, or is this it?"

"This is it," Victoria confirmed with an enigmatic smile. "I decided to keep this particular one small and . . . intimate. Now that everyone's here, I'll get the champagne and we can celebrate my announcement. Lydia, you and Kit bring the glasses in from the kitchen. They're in the upper cupboard to the right of the sink."

Kit watched as Stephen and Lydia exchanged uneasy glances. They were obviously worried about what Victoria had to say. And having experienced firsthand the older woman's penchant for stirring up trouble, Kit knew they probably had good reason to feel concerned. Then Lydia was on her feet, smiling companionably at Kit. "Shall we?"

"Somehow I was expecting a larger gathering," Kit remarked, glancing at Lydia inquiringly, once they were in the kitchen and loading the glasses onto a tray.

"Oh, no. Aunt Victoria said it would just be family." She threw Kit an impish look. "Does she know something I don't? Something worth celebrating with champagne?"

"No! It's nothing like that." Kit shook her head hastily, then quickly changed the subject. "Is this all your family? Stephen told me that his father died when he was just a baby, and that he'd lost his sister some years ago, but—'' She paused, suddenly realizing that she could be treading on delicate ground.

''It's all right, I don't mind your asking. Unfortunately this is everyone. My parents were killed in a plane crash when I was ten,'' Lydia replied easily. ''Aunt Victoria took me in and raised me after that. I'll never be able to thank her enough for the love and care she gave me.''

Kit blinked at that piece of information. It certainly didn't sound like the Victoria Stephen had described. But before she could comment, Lydia spoke again. ''Strange that Stephen should tell you about Carrie,'' she said, elaborating when she saw Kit's confused expression, ''Stephen's sister. She's sort of a taboo topic around here. I was just surprised that you knew about her.''

''They don't even discuss her with you?'' Kit asked hesitantly.

Lydia shook her head. ''I only knew of Carrie's existence because my parents mentioned her one time. Oh, well, I guess it doesn't matter anymore, does it?'' she said lightly, not expecting a response, and not realizing that she'd created more questions for Kit than she'd answered. ''You set? I'm dying to find out what Aunt Victoria's news is.''

As it turned out, Victoria St. Clair's tiny tidbit created an instant furor.

Stephen was the first to regain his voice. ''You've *what*?''

''You heard me.'' Victoria tossed her head back arrogantly, her dark eyes gleaming with the light of battle. ''I've sold it. Everything. The business, the apartment, the mansion. Everything.''

''Why?'' Stephen demanded, ignoring the restraining hand Kit put on his arm. ''Clairington meant the world to you. It was your life.''

Victoria stared down into the sparkling glass of champagne she held between tense white fingers. ''You seem angry, Stephen," she murmured with a touch of bewilderment that seemed totally foreign to her nature. "I'm surprised. I would have thought you'd be overjoyed to see me give it all up."

"Twenty years ago, I would have been," Stephen agreed bluntly. "But why now? It doesn't make sense."

For the first time, Peter spoke up, interrupting hesitantly. "I know I haven't been a member of this family for long, and excuse me if I seem too personal..." He cleared his throat awkwardly, pushing his large-framed glasses farther up on his nose. "There weren't any—er—health considerations in this decision, were there, Victoria?"

There was a moment of dead silence and Kit watched, wide-eyed, as every last vestige of color drained from Stephen's face. *Why, he really does care,* she realized with relief. Underneath all that anger and bitterness, he really loves his mother very much.

And then Victoria laughed, the sound surprisingly kind. "It's sweet of you to be concerned, Peter, but I'm not dying of some dread disease, if that's what you were thinking." She glanced toward Stephen and Kit, and for a split second Kit could have sworn she saw a desperate yearning in those black eyes. "Kit, pour Stephen some champagne. He's gone quite pale, poor boy."

Stephen was swift to recover, waving away the profered wine. "None for me. I'm beginning to think I'm going to need a clear head! You still haven't explained why you're doing this, Mother. The famous Victoria, the epitome of rich elegance and jet-set living, slumming? I mean, as charming as this house is, it isn't quite up to your usual standards."

"Perhaps you don't know me as well as you think, Stephen," Victoria countered with a sudden spurt of temper. "I'm not slumming, just taking the time to enjoy my family. Now that Lydia is settled and openly talking about having children, and you and Kit are practically on your honeymoon—'' Victoria broke off, her defiant eyes clashing with the thunderous expression in Stephen's. "You can deny there's anything serious between you and Kit until the cows come home, Stephen," Victoria declared aggressively, "but I do have eyes in my head, and though I may be a lot of things, I'm certainly not dull witted!" She shrugged carelessly. "Besides, what's wrong with wanting to spend time with you and Lydia and your children when you have them?"

"Why would you want to do that? You never had the urge before!"

"Stephen!" Both Kit and Lydia spoke at once.

Lydia jumped to her feet and rushed to her aunt's side, throwing her arms about the older woman. "Well, I, for one, am thrilled," she announced fiercely. "You've always been more like a mother to me than an aunt. Peter and I will be delighted to have you as a grandmother to our children."

"And you, Stephen, will you be delighted to have me as a grandmother to yours?" Victoria's voice was taunting.

"But of course, Mother," Stephen said blandly, inclining his golden head. "I await with bated breath the day my son has his first accident on your favorite designer dress."

"Do your really?" Victoria asked, an odd little smile playing around her mouth. "Would it amaze you to hear that I'm looking forward to it, as well?"

Stephen gave a bark of laughter. "Most assuredly!"

A sly gleam of amusement danced in Victoria's dark eyes. "Well, my dear boy, you provide me with a grandson and I'll be only too happy to donate my most expensive dress to the cause!" Impulsively she crossed to Stephen's side, sliding her hand through his arm as he stood up. "Truce?" she suggested. And at his nod, she turned to the others with a brilliant smile. "Come on, everyone. Let's have dinner. I'm starved!"

"I MADE A COMPLETE ass out of myself, didn't I?" Stephen said morosely when he finally pulled the car to a halt outside Kit's duplex.

"Giving Lydia a ten-minute standing ovation for stating her desire to stay home and raise the children she and Peter are planning, might have been a bit excessive," Kit agreed with a dry smile. "But insisting that it should be made into a constitutional amendment and demanding we immediately ratify it, was definitely going overboard."

"Oh, and I suppose reading quotes from *Women on the Rise: The Ten Best Methods for Controlling your Man* during dessert, isn't considered extreme?" he challenged indignantly. "Just out of curiosity, do you always carry that thing around in your purse with you?"

"Always," Kit stated firmly. She'd undergo torture before she'd admit that her flu-stricken neighbor, a feminist with some very peculiar notions regarding men, had begged Kit to return the long-overdue book to the library.

"I wish I'd had a camera." Stephen chuckled unexpectedly, shaking his head in disbelief. "The expression on Lydia's face when you read the chapter, 'Sexual Power over Men: More Inventive Uses for Chains' was classic. I thought Peter was going to have a stroke."

Kit slid down in her seat, blushing darkly at the memory. "It must have been all that champagne," she mumbled, not quite believing that she'd been so brazen.

"Speak for yourself. I remained stone-cold sober throughout!"

"Then what's your excuse?" Kit snapped pertly, before groaning, "Do you think your mother will ever speak to me again?"

"Speak to you? Are you kidding? She was cheering you on! I'm sure she thinks I've finally met my match."

"And have you?"

The tart question hung in the air between them, draining the laughter from Stephen's face.

"What you really mean is, have I changed my stance about a wife with a career," he replied, his eyes narrowing on her irritably. "I'd have thought the conversation at dinner tonight, amusing as it was, would have answered that question for you. No. I haven't changed my mind. Have you?"

Kit's chin lifted proudly. "No."

A number of conflicting emotions chased across Stephen's face, frustration uppermost. "There's one small detail you might want to take into consideration before you make such an unequivocal statement, my love."

"Which is?"

Stephen caught the back of Kit's head with his hand, pulling her roughly toward him. "Just this." And his lips closed passionately over hers.

"IF THIS LATEST FORMULA doesn't work, I don't know what will," Kit said with a sigh. "Which delectably disgusting creature do you want this time?"

"The Oozing Bloodsuckers." Todd's gray eyes gleamed rapaciously. "You can have the Slithering Serpents."

"Gee, thanks." Kit walked over to the light switch and with great deliberation flicked on the red warning light. "No screw-ups this time," she muttered. "No point in handing him an excuse to get rid of me."

She hadn't seen Stephen since the dinner at his mother's, when he had kissed her so heatedly, and then left her hungering for more. Six full days had passed without a word from him, not even the tiniest glimpse of his golden head to ease the intense longing that held her in its grip.

Well, if he thought she was going to make the first move, he was very much mistaken. She knew perfectly well what he was up to—trying to force her to choose between him and her job. Kit's mouth tightened. From now on she'd be cool and distant, the perfect professional, whenever he appeared. Besides, it was his turn to be driven insane. She was tired of it!

"Are you planning on standing there all day?" an annoyed Todd asked, interrupting her thoughts. "Or are we going to get the show on the road?" He glowered down at her from his superior height. "You aren't any fun anymore, Kit," he complained bitterly. "No explosions. No goofs. No special magic. In other words, kiddo—boring. What's with you these days, anyway?"

Kit turned to look at him, a defensive gleam in her golden-brown eyes. "What do you mean?"

"You know perfectly well what I mean," Todd retorted tautly, picking up the squirt guns and filling them with water, his movements unnaturally stiff. "One minute you're with me and the next you're off in your own little world. And don't try to tell me Mr. High and Mighty isn't responsible—" he cut Kit off forcefully when she opened her mouth to protest "—because I know better. Ever since you and St. Clair—" He stopped, his serious eyes noting the sudden vulnerability of Kit's delicately drawn features, the pain he read there totally defeating him. As much as he cared, it was all too obvious he hadn't a hope with Kit. The best he could do was be supportive—if it didn't kill him in the process!

"Damn office gossip, anyway." Todd exhaled sharply, regret tingeing his voice. "I'm sorry, Kit. I should keep my big mouth shut, I know, but I just can't help worrying about you." He hesitated, then added gruffly, "Look, if you ever feel the need to talk, kiddo, I've got big ears, a zipped lip and a ton of sympathy to spare."

"Thanks, Todd." Kit flashed him a swift, tremulous smile. "You're a good friend, but I can handle it. Really," she assured him gently, when he continued to frown.

Todd was right, Kit acknowledged. She had to shake off this lethargy. Her work was *not* going to suffer because of Stephen St. Clair. It would be the ultimate irony if that were to happen. With renewed determination, Kit turned back to the project before her. "Here's your pellet," she said briskly, handing Todd a small red ball. "Drop it in the gun and shake."

He studied her silently for a moment longer before obediently following her instructions. An unruly lock of black hair tumbled onto his forehead. "I've been looking forward to this all week." Todd sighed gustily. "I guess I'm just a child at heart."

"You and me both," Kit agreed, her concentration fixed on the small yellow ball she had dropped into her squirt gun. She shook it rapidly. "So far, so good," she murmured, squinting at the slowly thickening mixture.

A stream of bright red slime blasted past her left ear and, with a squeal, Kit ducked down behind the work table. "Hey, no fair!" she yelped, experiencing a heady thrill of exhilaration—something that had been sadly lacking in her life the past few days. Kit's spirits took flight. Just what the doctor ordered, she thought, her eyes gleaming mischievously—a nice, raucous water-pistol battle to drown out her blues!

She heard Todd's excited voice. "It's working, Kit! Come look."

She peeked suspiciously out from behind the table. "Not on your life!" She giggled, drawing back and scuttling around to the other end. "I'm not that gullible." She took rapid aim at Todd's crouched figure and squeezed the trigger, canary-yellow goo splattering on the wall just above his head.

Kit watched in delighted surprise as the thick mixture stuck there, bubbling revoltingly before slowly taking the shape of several intricately entwined snakes. A broad, triumphant grin spread across her face. They'd done it!

"Hey, Kit!"

Without thinking, Kit turned her head toward Todd's voice and received a faceful of Oozing Bloodsuckers for her trouble. "I'll get you for that, you sneak!" she roared through the bubbling, red mass. She heard Todd's snicker, followed immediately by the sound of the lab door opening and closing as he wisely decided to leave the immediate vicinity.

She waited patiently for the thick, wormy concoction to solidify against her skin before yanking it off and tossing it onto the worktable, intense satisfaction gleaming in her bright eyes. It worked! Stephen would be delighted. Then her expression sobered. Stephen. *Damn!*

"Miss Mallory?" Her name came crackling through the speaker of the intercom. "Is it safe to come in?" Kit's eyes widened. Well, speak of the devil.

She walked to the door, pulling it open, her eyes practically swallowing Stephen whole. *Well, so much for being cool and distant,* Kit thought derisively. Why didn't she just throw herself at his feet and be done with it? "All's clear." Kit forced out the bright words, pinning a friendly expression on her face as he ushered Lydia into the room ahead of him.

"I thought Lydia might be interested in seeing you in your natural setting," Stephen informed her, tongue in cheek. "She was a little reluctant after hearing about some of your more imaginative mishaps, but I convinced her you weren't working on anything too dangerous today."

Lydia gave her a weak smile. "You don't mind, do you?"

"No, of course not," Kit responded warmly, feeling a twinge of guilt at Lydia's understandable apprehension. The poor woman clearly didn't know what to expect after the strange way the dinner at Victoria's had ended—and Stephen was obviously taking advantage of that bewilderment. *The rat.*

She turned mocking gold eyes on Stephen. "The dynamite is all safely packed away and the nitro experiment was yesterday. All we have to work with today are slimy little bugs.'' She heard the quiet rumble of Stephen's laughter and swiftly lowered her lashes to conceal the answering gleam of amusement she knew must be sparkling in her eyes. Where had her anger gone, Kit wondered in amazement, her righteous indignation? One minute in his company and already they were attuned, their shared sense of humor an instant bond between them.

And suddenly that wasn't the only thing she wanted to share with him. Trying to conceal her inner elation, Kit pointed casually toward the lab wall. "There's a perfect example of one of our little projects," she said, addressing Lydia.

Following the movement of Kit's hand, Lydia drew back in nervous alarm, her eyes falling on the bright yellow lump decorating the wall. "Wh—what is it?" she asked faintly.

"A Slithering Serpent," Kit informed her with great relish, striding over to the rubbery creation and jerking it off the wall. "We've just today gotten the formula right so that we can squirt these little cuties from water pistols," she announced proudly, her eyes eagerly watching for Stephen's reaction.

It was everything she could have hoped for. "You've done it?" he demanded in astonishment, a wide, excited grin spreading across his face. He was at her side in an instant, sweeping her off her feet and twirling her around. "Congratulations! That's fantastic!" he crowed, hugging her tightly. He pulled back slightly to look down at her, and the warmth expressed in his sapphire eyes was echoed in his voice. "I knew you could do it, Kit. I never doubted you for a minute," he told her very softly, and very sincerely, before reluctantly releasing her.

Kit turned toward Lydia, Stephen's praise bubbling like champagne through her veins, the heat of his touch still branding her skin. "It's really great stuff," she enthused, so wrapped up in her pet project and her fevered reaction to Stephen that she didn't notice Lydia's less-than-thrilled response. "It's so simple to use—just drop the pellet in the water gun, shake and squirt away. It comes in four colors, and it's a dream to clean up. But the best part—"

Stephen laughed at her eagerness. "You're beginning to sound like a commercial."

"Well, that's because I'm so pleased with it. But the best part is that—"

"Hey, Kit!" Subconsciously she'd heard the lab door open behind her, but she'd been so caught up in her explanation about their latest invention, that she hadn't paid attention. Her reaction was pure instinct. She ducked.

"Oh!" Lydia shrieked.

Kit squeezed her eyes shut, wincing. *Oh, no!* Please don't let it have happened, she pleaded silently and forcefully. Oh, please let it be all right. She peeked up at Lydia from her crouched position and cringed. Nuts! Nuts! *Nuts!*

Bright red slime was oozing down the front of Lydia's cream-colored silk dress. The younger woman's face was paper-white, her mouth wide open, her bulging eyes glued to the repulsively pulsating glob rapidly spreading across her small, rounded breasts.

Kit leaped to her feet and attempted to calm the terrified woman. "Don't panic. It'll be okay, Lydia. See, it's all finished bubbling and I can take it off you now." She swiftly ripped the rubbery mass off the silk dress.

"It hasn't stained," Kit reassured her. "It's just one of those creatures I was telling you about." She dangled the quivering, red worms in front of a horror-stricken Lydia, desperate for a way to save the situation. "Look, they can't hurt you."

"Kit!" She heard Stephen's warning voice, but ignored it, concentrating on the shocked woman in front of her.

She offered her most brilliant smile. "See, it's an Oozing Bloodsucker. And watch this—" She popped the bright red worms into her mouth, her words garbled as she tried to speak around the wiggly mass. "They're even edible!"

"Ohh…" The sound escaped softly from Lydia's white lips before she slowly toppled backward in a dead faint.

CHAPTER NINE

"QUICK! Pull that chair over here!" Stephen roared at a gaping Kit and Todd. "Light as she is, I'm not Superman!" He spread his legs wide in an attempt to better balance himself beneath the dead weight in his arms.

Kit hurried to do as he ordered, still unable to believe Stephen had managed to catch Lydia before she hit the ground, his lightning-fast reflexes saving the young woman from a nasty fall.

"I'm sorry, Mr. St. Clair." Todd moaned abjectly, wringing his hands, clearly beside himself with horrified concern. "The red light was still on and I didn't see her there until after Kit had ducked. By then it was too—"

"Stow it, Templeton. Go get some water or something, will you?" Stephen cut Todd's apology off abruptly, as he carefully levered his unconscious cousin into the armchair Kit held for him. With a final worried glance at Lydia's still body, Todd vanished hastily through the door.

Stephen turned on Kit, swearing bitterly. "Did you have to eat them, for God's sake?" he demanded. "She would have been fine if you hadn't pulled that cute little stunt."

"I'm sorry," Kit murmured miserably, awkwardly patting Lydia's limp hand. "I didn't know what else to do. I thought it would help."

"Help?" he blasted her. "You almost had me right down there beside her when you put those slimy things in your mouth! You never told me they were edible!"

"They are *not* slimy!" She defended her invention indignantly, unthinkingly dropping Lydia's hand—and wincing at the resulting thud. "Actually they're chewy and they taste pretty good, too. The Oozing Bloodsuckers are cherry-flavored and the Slithering Serpents are lemon—"

"*Kit!*"

Her jaw jutted mutinously. Did he really think she had deliberately attempted to frighten his cousin? "I tried to tell you," Kit insisted, struggling to keep her voice from becoming belligerent, knowing his anger was really concern for Lydia. "But I kept getting interrupted."

They faced each other, the growing tension palpable between them.

"What's going on?" The lab door banged open behind them. "They told me something was wrong with Lydia." Victoria St. Clair appeared in the doorway, taking in the frozen scene before her in one swift glance. Spying Lydia slumped in the armchair, she gave a small cry of alarm and hurried over, stooping beside her unconscious niece. "Dear heavens, what's happened to her?" Victoria's eyes turned toward a guilt-ridden Kit and she groaned, her umber-tinted lids falling shut. "I might have known—I should have known!" she muttered under her breath, then asked tightly, "What have you done now, Kit?"

"What the hell do you think?" Stephen snapped before Kit could even open her mouth. "The same thing Calamity Jane, here, always does. She created as much of a furor as she could possibly manage in—believe it or not—under five minutes! I shudder to think what she'd have done if I'd given her ten!"

"Swearing, Stephen, is not going to help matters any. Nor will shouting into my ear. If you'd brought Lydia directly to the car as you were supposed to, instead of into this madhouse you're running, it never would have happened!" Victoria turned sharp black eyes on Kit, a scathing comment trembling on her lips. And then she sighed in defeat, shaking her head wearily. "What was it this time, Kit?" she asked in a resigned voice. "Poison? Gas? Or perhaps one of your more inventive accidents?"

"Worms." Kit choked out the word, wretchedly. Would she never appear in a good light before Stephen and his family? "It was the worms that did it to her."

Victoria cleared her throat. "Worms?"

"Enough, Mother! This isn't the time for a postmortem," Stephen added, interrupting Kit's incoherent attempts to explain. "Wait in the car if you can't be of any help and I'll bring Lydia out as soon as she comes to," Stephen ordered harshly.

"You mean *if* she comes to," Victoria retorted dryly. "Perhaps some water?"

As though on cue, Lydia began to stir in the chair, drawing their attention as her dark lashes fluttered faintly against her pale cheeks. Abruptly her eyes few open, panic mirrored in their glassy depths. "Stephen," she moaned.

"I'm here, sweetheart."

"What happened?" Lydia whispered. "I can't remember—" Her eyes fell on Kit and she gasped, cowering against the chair, her slender body beginning to tremble helplessly. "She ate them, Stephen," she cried hysterically and burst into frantic, uncontrollable sobs. "Those disgusting worms! She put them in her mouth!"

"Kit, disappear," Stephen ordered summarily, kneeling beside his distraught cousin, gathering her up into his protective embrace. "Go find the rock Templeton's crawled under and the pair of you vanish until five o'clock. Then I want you both in my office." Kit swallowed convulsively and nodded, backing away from the painful scene before her. She felt totally, horribly alone, and not even the sympathetic glance Victoria spared her, eased her distress. "And Kit?" She froze. "If you want to come out of this with a whole skin, you won't be late."

KIT AND TODD stood outside Stephen's office, each looking at the other for some much-needed emotional support. The building was totally deserted; everyone had already left for the weekend. Everyone, that is, except them.

"What's the time now?" Kit whispered.

"Two minutes later than two minutes ago."

"I think that's close enough. Go ahead and knock," she urged him.

"He said five o'clock and, knowing St. Clair, he meant five o'clock, not five minutes to. You knock if you're so eager to see him."

"You're being ridiculous!" she hissed at him. "Better that we're early than late. We've already been standing here for ten minutes debating the issue!"

"Please," Stephen requested with exaggerated politeness. Kit and Todd jumped at the word, having been so involved in their quiet argument that they hadn't heard the door open. "The suspense of waiting to see which of you would finally give in and knock on the damned door is killing me. Do come in!"

Kit smiled weakly, forcing her reluctant limbs to propel her forward. Where had the loving man of the past two months gone? she wondered unhappily. He clearly wasn't here—this remote iceman was a frighteningly cold, frighteningly familiar stranger. One she had known in another lifetime and would have been quite pleased to have never run into again. The door slammed closed behind them and the sound seemed like a death knell to an overly imaginative Kit.

"Sit." He barked the order and Kit and Todd instantly complied, relieved to find themselves seated on chairs and not on the floor. Stephen strode over to the window, his back to them, his hands folded across his broad chest. There was a stiff twitch to his shoulders and Kit could see the tight control he was maintaining on his temper.

"Mr. Templeton."

Todd quailed before the cutting tone, clearing his throat uncomfortably. "Yes, sir."

"That was not the brightest stunt I've seen you perform."

"No, sir. I'm sorry, sir."

Stephen turned to confront them, a weary, frustrated expression on his face. "Nor was it totally your fault. I have to assume some responsibility, since I was the one to allow Lydia into the insane asylum we laughingly call a laboratory, while an experiment was in progress."

"Sir?"

Stephen flashed Todd an irritated glance. "I'd appreciate a personal apology from you to Mrs. Vallance. Beyond that, I realize you and Kit were in the middle of one of your projects. The warning light was on and you weren't to know we were in the, ah, line of fire."

"No, sir."

Stephen sighed. "Get out of here, Templeton."

"Yes, sir!"

He waited until the door banged closed behind Todd's escaping figure before turning to Kit. "Miss Mallory."

"Yes, Mr. St. Clair?" Kit peeped up at him from beneath long, dark lashes. Perhaps things weren't as serious as she had first thought, considering Stephen's relatively mild annoyance with Todd. Her soft lips quivered into a hesitant, placatory smile. "Stephen?"

"Don't 'Stephen' me!" he blasted her coldly. "You can't win me over with a sweet little smile and a coy flutter of lashes."

She blinked at him in dismay. "I wasn't trying to—"

"Oh, no?" he interrupted in cynical disbelief. "Tell me what you were doing, if it wasn't using our relationship to get yourself out of your latest jam."

"Is that what you really think?" Kit questioned incredulously, her eyes beginning to flash with temper. "Surely you know me better than that. Besides, it was Todd who squirted Lydia, not me. I admit I didn't improve the situation any when I ate those worms, but I honestly thought it would help.'' She stared up at him from the chair with a pleading, conciliatory look. ''Come on, Stephen, aren't you overreacting just a little?''

It was absolutely, positively the wrong thing to say.

''Overreacting!'' He yanked her to her feet, giving her a hard shake when she struggled against his grip. ''You're not a child anymore, Kit. You can't point the finger at Todd and say 'he did it—it's not my fault.' This isn't a game, it's real life, with real-life, adult responsibilities to go along with it.''

''Do you think I don't know that?'' she spat back at him, fighting free of his hold, defiance in every line of her body. ''I wasn't blaming Todd. You yourself admitted that it was an accident. You don't believe I would have done anything to deliberately hurt Lydia, do you?''

''No, Kit. I don't.'' The fury drained from him, replaced by something close to disappointment. ''You still don't get it, do you, sweetheart?'' He exhaled roughly. ''Todd is not the head of the department, you are. Therefore, what happens in that department is your responsibility. True, Todd didn't show the best sense in the world when he burst into the room, firing away. But who is it that not only allows, but openly encourages that sort of—of laissez-faire attitude?'' His anger began to grow anew at the gleam of resentment he saw in her eyes.

''Dammit, Kit! Have you even bothered to say you're sorry? Did you even once think to ask how Lydia is doing?'' he castigated her in disgust. ''That poor girl was physically ill—physically ill,'' he stressed bitingly, ''in reaction to what you regard as an amusing little incident. Lydia's not like you, Kit. She doesn't make a habit of eating worms and blowing up labs and ambushing people with missiles! Things that seem to be everyday occurrences for you are a little out of her realm of experience. And what happened today completely terrified her!''

''I'm—I'm sorry.'' She stumbled over the words. ''I didn't—''

''And don't you *dare* tell me you didn't think!'' he bellowed furiously. ''Your actions since coming to work at this company have been inexcusable. Absolutely inexcusable,'' he repeated savagely, when she would have protested.

Kit hung her head, shame coursing through her. Stephen was right. She *had* allowed an increasingly lax attitude to prevail in the lab, enjoying the freedom it gave to experiment. But there was a difference between creating an imaginative environment in which to work and permitting the lunacy that had resulted instead. Certainly it shouldn't have gone to the extent of adversely affecting the general safety of those around her.

Kit nibbled painfully on her lower lip. It was her responsibility to enforce the proper atmosphere. Her job had become so pleasurable that she'd forgotten that that was what it was—a job. And Stephen had been fairly easy on her, all things considered. The majority of employers wouldn't have been so condoning. Far easier to cut her loose than risk any further, potentially more litigious, incidents.

But Stephen wasn't finished reprimanding her. ''And I think you can take a fairly accurate stab at why I've tolerated the hassle of keeping you on as an employee.'' Kit froze as Stephen's voice continued brutally, ''Unfortunately having an affair with the boss does not guarantee employment if you can't do a proper job.''

Her head shot up at that. ''We are not having an affair!'' she denied in a panic, his unwarranted attack ripping painfully through her. ''I'm good at my job, that's why you've kept me on. Our relationship has nothing whatsoever to do with it!''

"Doesn't it?" Stephen muttered. "Sometimes I wonder." He sighed, his anger abruptly draining away. He ran a hand through his hair and downward, massaging the tense muscles at the back of his neck. "I'm sorry, Kit. I suppose that was going a little too far. If it weren't for this—this excess of enthusiasm of yours, I'd say you were practically perfect."

"Would you?" Kit felt inordinately pleased.

Seeing her budding grin, he moved toward her, closing the space that separated them. "That doesn't change my anger over this incident, Kit," Stephen informed her sternly. He caught her hands in his and pulled her toward him until their bodies were just barely touching.

"I shouldn't be doing this, but I can't seem to resist." His expression was almost grim. "You drive me to distraction, Kit. Having you even this near to me—I can't think straight. There's something about you that calls to me, pulls me to you. Sometimes I wonder if you aren't a siren beckoning me to my doom."

All Kit's defenses fell before the helpless sincerity in his voice. "If that's true," she had to respond, shaken by his words, "then it's a doom we share." She became more shaken when he continued.

"Even the times we're apart, I find I can't concentrate, can't work, because I'm unable to get you out of my thoughts. I catch myself remembering the strangest things. Things like the sweet fragrance of your hair, the dark gold of your eyes—" his voice deepened "—the honeyed warmth of your lips parting beneath mine."

Kit trembled in his arms, his words kindling a blaze within her that was rapidly burning out of control—and the strength of her feelings frightened her. "Stephen," she choked out, her voice barely audible. "Why are you doing this? Is this your way of punishing me because of Lydia?" She pushed her hands against the hard-muscled wall of his chest, only to have them trapped there. Then his arms tightened gently around her, and he laughed quietly.

"Does this feel like a punishment to you? If feels more like heaven to me." He drew her unresisting body closer still, cradling her against him until they fit as one. He touched her hair, easing the silky strands free of their braid and fanning the tawny curtain around her shoulders. "Would you like to know what I'm imagining right now?" he murmured against the gleaming tresses.

"Will I regret it if I say yes?" Kit asked nervously in return.

Stephen smiled at her uncharacteristic hesitation. "Remember that first time in my office, when we ended up on the floor, with you trapped against my back? I can't seem to get that memory out of my mind. You were so horrified, caught there. And I was so very angry. I wish—I wish it could happen all over again. I know what I'd do differently."

Kit's lips parted, a tiny gasp escaping her lungs, her heart pounding in her chest so rapidly she could scarcely force out her question. "What? What would you do differently?"

"This." His mouth lightly touched hers, nibbling her lips gently before slowly easing away. "Would I have shocked you, if I'd kissed you like that?"

"Yes." Kit's tongue darted out, touching where his had touched, shyly retreating when Stephen's blue eyes darkened at her action. "But it would have been a very nice sort of shock," she admitted, flushing slightly at her candor. She could tell her answer had pleased him, for a half smile relaxed his face.

"And if, instead, I'd—" Stephen's lips brushed her ear, sending a shudder through her as he whispered his suggestion into the shell-like hollow, laughing in delight when a delicate pink suffused her skin.

His words conjured up such a vivid image that Kit could actually see it before her, and her nerves began to tingle, quivering with a strange, urgent need. "I wouldn't have let you," she breathed in a husky voice.

But there was a wistful yearning growing in her golden-brown eyes, and suddenly, more than anything, Stephen wanted to satisfy that need. He wanted to cherish her, fulfill her and care for her in a way she'd never known before. "Kit," he coaxed gently, cupping her rounded chin in the palm of his hand, his eyes speaking to her more clearly than any words could. "Let me show you how much you mean to me. Let me give you a small piece of the love I feel for you."

Kit stared up at Stephen, overwhelmed by his admission, unable to say a word and yet wanting to respond in a way he'd understand. Slowly, she moved against him, her face lifted toward his, her hands sliding lightly across the angled bones of his jawline. She pulled his head down to meet hers, her lips parting instinctively beneath the firm onslaught of his mouth.

It was a moment out of time. A moment of giving and taking and sharing. A moment that spoke of love and commitment. Never had Kit experienced such fulfillment and she prayed with all her heart that Stephen felt the same. And when he reluctantly released her, she knew by his expression that he did.

"More than anything in the world, I'd like to make love to you right this minute." He touched a finger to her lips before she could speak. "No. Don't say anything, Kit. Because if you said yes, I wouldn't have the strength to resist you. And if you said no, I'd only want to try to change your mind."

Kit turned her head slightly, rubbing her cheek against his finger. "But doesn't it—doesn't it occur to you that by saying yes, I might not want you to resist?" she dared to ask.

"Oh, yes, my love, it most definitely occurs to me," Stephen groaned, lowering his head to avoid her eyes. "And—" he hesitated an instant "—and by saying no?" he finally asked in a husky voice.

Kit licked her suddenly dry lips. "And by saying no, that—that I might secretly be hoping you'd try to change my mind."

A warm, beautiful smile lit his face. "Thank you, sweetheart. I can't tell you how happy that knowledge makes me. But I know you too well to even attempt such a thing." He raised intense blue eyes to her flushed face, his fingers moving lazily from her cheek toward her temple. Then his hand slid into her hair, tucking the silky strands behind one ear. He could feel her tremble against him, and knowing how much his touch disturbed her, he reluctantly put a little space between them.

"Stephen?" Kit murmured in confusion when he moved away.

His lips twisted. "I'm sorry, Kit," he said, attempting a light tone. "You've been so sweet, I don't dare stay too close." Then, more seriously, he continued, "And as much as I'd love to take advantage of the situation, we have too much to discuss, too much that's keeping us apart, to make that sort of mistake."

"Would it be such a mistake?" Kit had to try one last time, a little hurt that he thought so.

Stephen shut his eyes, struggling for control. "Yes," he finally said, though she could hear the frustration in his voice. "It would be if we didn't consider all the consequences."

"And there would be consequences," Kit stated wryly.

"There would be consequences," Stephen concurred. "Not least of which could be a pregnancy. Not that I wouldn't be delighted to have my child growing within you. In fact, it tempts me no end to use that as a way to bend you to my way of thinking. But I couldn't do that to you. You'd hate me for it afterward, and I think in time, I'd hate myself. Besides," he added grimly, "I have a feeling I'd be putting myself on the same level as Jeffery, if I took advantage of you like that."

Kit was shocked. "No, Stephen! Why would you think that? You're nothing like Jeffery." In fact, she couldn't think of anyone more totally different. "Jeffery wanted one thing, and one thing only." A dark red stain swept up Kit's cheeks, but she forced herself to be brutally honest. "If I had offered myself to him, the way I just did to you, he would never have—have—"

"Have said no?" Kit nodded, not quite able to meet Stephen's eyes.

"Fortunately we didn't quite get to the point of a full-blown affair." More than fortunate. It was an immense relief to Kit that she'd never given in to Jeffery's attempts to put their relationship on a more intimate footing. Jeffery had been a user, out for what he could get. And he'd wanted Kit. If she'd been just a little bit older, she would have realized that much sooner than she had. As it was, she was lucky to have escaped relatively unscathed.

"You're too generous, Kit," Stephen said wryly. "Don't you think it shows some major flaw in my character that I'd consider using a pregnancy to force you to my will?"

Kit looked at him uncertainly. "You wouldn't really do that, would you?"

"If you mean would I insist we marry if I made you pregnant, then, yes I would. And if you mean would I insist you quit work, then, yes to that, too. But I would also love you with all my heart and care for you and cherish you." His sapphire-blue eyes pleaded with her. "Wouldn't that be enough? Couldn't you be satisfied with that?"

Yes, I could! Kit shook her head to clear the subversive thought and stepped back a pace, needing to put more distance between them. His presence was too potent, too overpowering. She couldn't think straight when he was so near. "At one time, if a man had said that to me, I think I would have jumped at the offer."

"You mean Jeffery, don't you?" Stephen frowned harshly, not liking the implication. "If Jeffery had been free, and had asked you to marry him, would you have?"

"Yes," Kit answered simply. "But it wouldn't have lasted because he didn't really love me—and I've since discovered that what I felt for him wasn't love, either. I allowed him to dictate who and what I was. But I refuse to make that same mistake again. How can you truly love someone when you're constantly trying to change them?"

"I assume that little speech is aimed at me," Stephen commented tightly, a sharp edge in his voice. "You think that by loving my wife and insisting on the best possible life for my children, I'd be trying to change them?"

A stubborn gleam entered Kit's eyes. "If you force them to be something they're not, then you don't really love them."

Stephen was instantly by her side, reaching out to touch her, and then hesitating. "Kit, I do love you, more than you can possibly know. I want you to be my wife. I want to be married to you and spend the rest of my life with you."

"Oh, Stephen," Kit cried softly, a great sadness filling her eyes. "How can you say you love me when you want to put conditions on that love? You don't want the total me, you want bits and pieces that fit into your concept of a wife and mother. But I can't become something I'm not. Not just to suit your convenience."

"You're twisting things around!"

Kit shook her head. "No, I don't think I am. I love my job, but you want to take that away from me. You say that a wife having a career isn't compatible with your image of family life. So you want to wipe out a whole portion of what makes me who I am, just so I'll fit into this dream you wish to fulfill."

"You're putting your career ahead of me when you say that," he stated bitterly.

"And you act jealous of my work! Are you?" she demanded incredulously. He made a small impatient gesture that Kit took to be a denial. "Yet you seem to think that I have to choose one or the other, that I can't have both. You seem to think that by wanting to work, I'm saying I don't want you. That's ridiculous. You'd always be number one in my life."

"I know firsthand that it wouldn't work, Kit," Stephen informed her coldly. "You can't be an effective wife and mother when your career is of such paramount importance."

"Your mother couldn't! Your mother was the one who wasn't an effective mother!" Kit exploded, pushed beyond caution. "She was the one who couldn't successfully combine the two. You can't use her to judge me. It's not fair! You want me to stay home and mind the children because you and your sister were neglected by your mother. That *is* what you're saying, isn't it? Well, thank you so very much, but I am *not* your mother. I would always put you and any children we had ahead of my job. But you refuse to believe that. You're totally blind to any possibility other than the one you're clinging to so determinedly."

"I don't think you're the same as my mother!" Stephen shot back. "If I did, I wouldn't love you the way I do."

"Stephen, you're not making any sense," Kit sighed, totally frustrated by the sheer illogic of his statements. "The whole reason you want me to stay at home is that Victoria didn't. Then you admit I'm not anything like your mother. You can't have it both ways. Either I'm a dedicated career woman like Victoria, who will neglect you and the little ones because of a love affair with my job and a lack of love for you, or I'm a woman who loves you first and foremost and will always put my family ahead of my job. Well, which is it? To be perfectly honest, I'm getting a little confused here.''

Stephen turned his back on her, his tension revealed by the rigidity of his shoulders. ''I can only repeat what I believe to be true—that it is in the best interest of the children that their mother be at home to care for them.''

''And that's all you're willing to say? There's no further discussion, and no reprieve?'' At his silence, Kit closed her eyes in defeat. So be it. She couldn't live the way he wanted her to. She couldn't pretend to be the person he seemed to need so desperately. It would only lead to disaster.

''I don't agree with you, Stephen. And I don't see how we can ever hope to come to terms with any of it when we're so opposed in our beliefs.'' She paused, hoping he'd respond to that. But a response never came. Then, taking a deep breath, she said, ''I'll send my formal resignation to Miss Dobson. I'm sure you understand why I can't continue working for you.''

Kit waited for a long moment, waited for him to say something, waited for him to say anything that would save the situation. But the wait was in vain. He didn't say a word. He didn't even turn around to look at her as she quietly left the room.

CHAPTER TEN

SHE'D QUIT! She'd actually gone and quit. Kit sat on her living-room couch, staring into space, numbed. No job to return to Monday morning, no lab experiments, no fun little toys to tinker with, but far worse—no Stephen. She glanced out the window, noticing for the first time that the sun must have set long ago. It was pitch-black outside. And suddenly Kit realized how exhausted she was, feeling physically as well as emotionally drained.

Wearily she wandered into her room, throwing herself facedown on the bed, not bothering to change out of her clothes or pull back the bedspread. He hadn't even protested when she'd quit. Not one little word had he uttered to try to stop her. Kit closed her eyes against the tears that threatened to fall, refusing to give in to them. The least he could have done was to turn around and look at her. Not doing so seemed a horribly symbolic gesture. And with that depressing thought, she was asleep.

The next few days passed in a haze as Kit tried to decide what she wanted to do. But it was as though her brain had turned itself off. A voice inside her head kept talking, giving her instructions, but the connection didn't work properly, nothing was getting through. Finally one small word made itself heard—home.

Without conscious decision, Kit packed her bags, loaded the car and seated herself behind the steering wheel of her Honda compact. She didn't remember a thing about the long drive to Pasadena. Nor did she remember parking her car in the driveway and carrying her luggage to the front of the house. All she knew was that when she realized her surroundings, she was standing in front of her parents' door with her fist raised, ready to hammer on the wooden surface.

Kit nibbled her lip in dismay. How in the world was she going to explain her presence? she wondered. She squirmed a little, realizing she'd have to make a clean breast of things. Perhaps she could say something like "the engagement's off, but don't worry, it was never really on in the first place." Or maybe she could tell them that Stephen had wanted her to quit her job, and have his babies. So she'd quit her job, because he'd made such an insulting offer, and now she wouldn't be having *anyone's* babies.

The front door opened.

"Hello there, Kitten. Thought that was your car. Were you planning on coming in or would you like to stand out there a while longer?"

Kit stood staring at her father for a full second before his teasing words sank in. Carefully she lowered her fist. "The engagement's off," she blurted out. "But don't worry, it was never really on in the first place. Stephen wanted me to quit my job and have his babies, but I didn't want to. So—so I quit my job."

"But no babies?" Christopher questioned gravely, patting his pockets in search of his pipe. "Seems the least he could have done was throw in the babies, since you were gracious enough to quit your job."

Kit shook her head. "No, no babies." And promptly burst into tears.

"Poor little girl." Christopher put his arms around his daughter, hugging her gently. "Why don't I bring in your bags while you go find your mother and tell her what's happened. You know you're welcome to stay as long as you want."

"Thanks, Dad," Kit murmured with a watery smile. "Have I told you recently how much I appreciate you and Mom? If I haven't, I—I'm sorry."

She found her mother a few minutes later, out in the farthest corner of the yard, weeding the flower bed. Elizabeth sat back on her heels at Kit's approach, raising a hand to shade her eyes.

."Why, hello, sweetie." She smiled affectionately, a touch of sympathy in her eyes when she saw Kit's woebegone expression. "Confession time, is it?"

Kit hesitated, confusion uppermost. "Sorry?"

Elizabeth stripped off her gardening gloves, patting the grass at her side. "Sit down, Kit. I thought maybe you'd come home to tell us the truth about your engagement to Stephen. Something along the lines of 'we aren't really getting married. Stephen just said that on the spur of the moment to get us out of an awkward moment.'" She raised an eyebrow inquiringly, waiting for Kit to speak. "No?"

"No. I mean, yes, but I didn't actually come home to confess—" Kit closed her mouth abruptly and sank beside her mother. "You knew all along we weren't engaged?" she asked, unable to hide her surprise.

Elizabeth frowned. "Kit, your father and I aren't that naive," she rebuked mildly. "It was very gallant of Stephen to try to ease you out of your predicament with his announcement. But I must say I'm a little disappointed in your handling of the matter since then."

"You mean, for not coming clean sooner?" At her mother's nod, Kit sighed. "You're right and I'm sorry, Mom. Things have been so mixed up the past couple of months that I've found myself doing a lot of things I'll probably regret later." Probably regret! Definitely regret and regret now, not later. *Minor* little things—like being so incredibly stubborn, like quitting her job so precipitately, like leaving Stephen.

"You're in love with him, aren't you?"

Kit caught her lip between her teeth. *It hurt so much.*
She didn't realize she'd said the words aloud until her
mother put an arm around her shoulder, urging her to her
feet.

"I know, darling. These things always do." She brushed
the bits of grass and leaves from her pants, announcing
briskly, "Time for some tea and sympathy. Maybe things
aren't totally hopeless."

It felt good to pour her heart out to her mother, to air all
her various woes. And Elizabeth was a good audience,
content to listen without judging or sermonizing.

When Kit finally came to the end of her story, Elizabeth commented, "I think it was smart that you and Stephen allowed your relationship to develop before
confronting this career issue. People are a lot more willing to compromise with someone they love."

Kit played with the handle of her teacup. "But he *isn't*
willing to compromise. When it comes right down to it, he
hasn't changed his opinion about career women one iota."
She roughly shoved her cup of tea to one side. "He knows
how important my career is to me, but he just doesn't
care."

Elizabeth ignored the petulant note in her daughter's
voice. "It's definitely a problem, Kit," she admitted. "It
sounds as if you two have backed each other into a corner, with neither one willing to give a little. Tell me this. Is
marriage to Stephen what you really want?"

Kit didn't need to say a word; her expression said it all.
She wanted him, all right. It was the easiest thing in the
world to picture herself married to Stephen, and the picture took Kit's breath away—especially when she added
some blond, blue-eyed mischiefmakers to the scene.

"Mmm. I rather thought as much," her mother murmured dryly. "It seems you have a choice to make. And I
don't envy your having to make it. If Stephen absolutely

refuses to give in, even a little, you'll probably have to choose between marriage to him and your career.''

"I want both!''

Elizabeth shook her head sadly. "We can't always have it all.''

"Do you think I haven't thought about saying to hell with my career and just marrying him?'' Kit demanded. "I've thought of nothing else. But what happens five or ten years down the road? Will I end up resenting him for forcing me to make such a choice? It's something that would always stand between us.''

"Marriage doesn't come with guarantees, Kit,'' Elizabeth pointed out gently. "You could have your career and still run into serious problems five or ten years down the road. And, unfortunately, Stephen's problem sounds as if it originates in his childhood and in his relationship with his mother. That isn't an easy situation to overcome.''

"But doesn't he understand that I'm not like his mother? I wouldn't neglect him or our children for my career!''

"I know that and you know that,'' Elizabeth agreed soothingly. "Try giving him some time to come to terms with it. From what you've told me, he was extremely distraught when Lydia fainted. Obviously he's very fond of his cousin, protective of her. Lydia's reaction undoubtedly threw him, and he overreacted. Once he's calmed down and thought about it for a while, maybe he'll be willing to meet you halfway.'' She fixed her gaze on Kit, her expression serious. "But, Kitten, you'll have to do some compromising, too. That's what marriage is about— at least a successful marriage. Lots of love, with a lot more compromise.''

OVER THE NEXT few days, Kit reflected on what her mother had said. Her parents were tactful enough to leave her alone, which gave her plenty of time to think. And think she did, all the while counting the hours and the days as they dragged by. She also gave serious consideration to what she'd do if Stephen refused to relent.

Was her career more important than her love for Stephen? Kit shook her head grimly. Of course it wasn't. Although her continuing to work seemed to be the main issue, in a strange way, it wasn't. It was really Stephen's willingness, or rather unwillingness, to put his prejudices and childhood resentments to one side and give her a chance. If only he would love and trust her enough to try, she knew she could prove she had her priorities straight, that she wouldn't abandon him or their children in favor of her job.

But was he willing to try? Did he really love her? The question gnawed at Kit. And as each successive day passed, she became more and more despondent, convinced that if he really cared, he'd have already contacted her.

It was a Saturday morning, two weeks after her blowup with Stephen, when Kit realized she'd have to come to a decision, and soon. She lay on the lawn in her parents' backyard, looking up at the blue sky, sucking on a blade of grass. Monday morning she'd have to either look for a new job—after all, she couldn't continue sponging off her parents, sweet as they'd been about it—or she'd have to confront Stephen. The problem was—which?

Kit shook her head. There was no problem. She'd known all along which she'd choose.

"Kit! Telephone!"

Kit's heart stood still. It had to be Stephen! He hadn't given up after all. The blade of grass dropped from her mouth and she was on her feet, racing across the yard toward the house. Her mother handed Kit the phone with an encouraging smile, discreetly shutting the door of the small study behind her as she left.

This was it. Kit wiped her damp hands down the side of her jeans and took a deep breath to calm herself. Slowly she raised the receiver to her ear. "Hello?" She winced at the nervous, quavery sound that emerged from her throat.

"'Lo yourself, kiddo. What's shaking?"

"Oh, it's you."

"Well, thanks a lot!" Todd retorted indignantly. "Some greeting that is—'oh, it's you.' Let me tell you, it's going to be a pretty cold day before I—"

"I'm sorry, Todd," Kit cut in hastily, struggling to conceal her disappointment. A reluctant smile touched her mouth. "It really is good to hear your voice."

"I should think so! Do you know what I had to go through to get this number? Your parents are unlisted, in case you didn't know."

"Are they? I hadn't realized." She frowned, suddenly curious. "How *did* you get the number?"

"And well you should ask!" Todd was in his element. Kit could just picture him rubbing his hands together, his mischievous gray eyes aglow. "It wasn't easy. I had to sneak into Miss Dobson's files and get it from your employment record. Almost got caught, too. If I hadn't had the presence of mind to let those rats loose—"

"You didn't!"

"I did. And I'm glad I did, too. You wouldn't believe some of the fascinating little tidbits they have in here. Makes really interesting reading."

Kit heard the rustle of papers. "I know I shouldn't fall for this. What did you find?" she asked resignedly, and then turned bright red when he told her. "They wouldn't put that in my personnel file! You're pulling my leg, Todd."

"Gospel truth," Todd declared. "Would you care to verify the info for me?" When she remained silent, he laughed. "Thought not. Oh, well, it was worth a try." Then he asked in a more serious voice, "So tell me what's going on, kiddo. You can't believe the stories I've been hearing. Scuttlebutt has it you were canned, but word from on high is that you're just on vacation. Considering that little incident with the worms, I found the vacation story a little hard to swallow. Sorry, bad pun. So I thought I'd get an answer straight from the horse's mouth. Spill it—what's going on?''

"You have such a flattering way of putting things, Todd,'' Kit informed him acidly. "I wasn't fired and I'm not on vacation. I quit.''

There was a long moment of silence, and then she heard Todd swear softly. "It's because of him, isn't it? This is all his fault.''

"No, Todd, you're wrong.''

"Am I?'' She'd never heard Todd so incensed. "He's been out to get you from the start! And now he's succeeded.''

"I'm the one who quit. He didn't—''

"I have eyes in my head, Kit! Do you really think I haven't noticed how things are between you two? The whole company's been gossiping about it for months.''

"Weeks.''

"Weeks. Don't sidetrack me. I'm serious.'' And he was. "Kit, it's tearing me up inside. I—I care about you, kiddo. I can't stand the thought of that—that—'' He forcibly bit back the imprecation. "Oh, dammit, Kit. I just don't want you hurt.''

Kit knew then. She supposed, if she'd really thought about it, she'd known all along. But she'd been too involved in her stormy relationship with Stephen to really pay attention. Why, even Stephen had been aware of Todd's feelings for her, remembering some of the little hints he'd dropped about Todd's protectiveness.

"I'm so sorry, Todd,'' she told him gently. "I don't know what to say.''

He was silent for a minute. "Gave it away, did I?'' he asked in a subdued voice. Then the old, cocky Todd reasserted himself. "Oh, well. Don't feel bad, kiddo. It's actually a relief to have it out in the open. I've always known it was a lost cause. The only man you've ever had eyes for was St. Clair—not that he appreciates it.''

''Todd—''

''Sorry. What are you going to do now? Any way you can unquit, and come back to work?''

''I—I don't think so.''

Todd sighed, a deep regretful sigh. ''You know I'll always be there for you, if you need me. I've got nice, broad shoulders, just perfect for crying on. Of course, being such a pip-squeak, you'd need a stepladder to reach them.''

Laughter at Todd's insane sense of humor mingled with the tears that pricked her eyes. ''Thank you, Todd,'' Kit murmured huskily. ''That means a lot to me.''

''It's nothing.'' There was an awkward silence, then briskly he said, ''Well, goodbye, kiddo. Take care of yourself. And promise me you'll stay in touch.''

''I promise,'' Kit whispered, and then the line went dead.

The tears that wouldn't come before, came now. Why did life have to be so complicated? Why couldn't it have been Todd she fell in love with, instead of Stephen? Kit searched for a box of Kleenex and blew her nose, mopping up the tears that didn't want to stop.

''Kit?'' It was her mother.

Kit swiftly wiped the remaining dampness from her cheeks, hoping her reddened eyes weren't too obvious to her keen-eyed mother. ''It was Todd, my co-worker at The Toy Company,'' she explained.

''Oh, I'm sorry, Kitten. I was hoping...''

Kit offered her mother a brave little smile. ''Me, too.'' She headed for the door, knowing she couldn't continue this conversation for much longer without bursting into tears again. ''Think I'll go enjoy some more of that sunshine. It's supposed to rain tomorrow.''

Kit returned to the backyard, surprised that she hadn't beaten a path through the grass, she'd come this way so often. She wrapped her arms around her waist, wishing they were Stephen's arms, wishing she could turn the clock back and start over with him. She loved him. She loved him more than anything in the world. Certainly more than her career.

If Stephen was so opposed to her working, then she wouldn't work. There were plenty of things she could do to keep herself happy and involved in the community. Undoubtedly she'd miss her job and the people she'd grown to like so well, but her mother was right. Someone had to compromise. And if, on this issue, she was the one who had to do it, then she would.

"Oh, Stephen," she whispered urgently, *"please still love me.* Please don't have given up on us. Because I don't think I could bear it if you have."

And then, as though in answer to her plea, she heard his voice.

"Hello, Kit."

For a moment Kit couldn't move. Every sense, every particle in her body was bursting into life and responding to Stephen's voice with an intensity that left her breathless. He'd come! As though in response to her despair, he'd come to her.

Slowly Kit turned to face him, wondering if he was aware of the effect he had on her. She could feel the heat in her cheeks and the trembling of her hands. A sweet, sharp joy filled her, sparkling in her golden eyes, reflecting her every thought and emotion. She hadn't a hope of hiding how she felt about him now, and suddenly she didn't want to. She wanted him to know that she loved him.

Stephen stepped closer in response, and then stopped, his face endearingly vulnerable, filled with an uncharacteristic hesitancy. But Kit felt no such hesitancy. She ran toward him, practically throwing herself against him, reveling in the strength of the arms Stephen wrapped around her. His hands crept up along her back until they cupped her head, cradling her against his chest. The rapid thud of his heart filled her ears and was echoed by her own.

They stood quietly for a long time, just holding each other, afraid to speak, afraid to break the tenuous closeness with words. It was enough that Stephen had come. All the hurt of the past days faded before that fact. And then he kissed her, a gentle, tender kiss that helped heal her heartache more completely than any wild, impassioned embrace could have.

Reluctantly Kit stirred in his arms. "Hello, yourself," she murmured, repeating his rather prosaic greeting into Stephen's shirt. She peeked up at him. "So much for my poor, tattered dignity. That wasn't exactly a standoffish reaction, was it?"

Stephen chuckled. "No, it wasn't, thank you very much. I couldn't have asked for a more satisfactory welcome." He rested his cheek against the top of her head with a sigh. "I missed you, sweetheart. You should never have quit. It made these past two weeks pure hell." Feeling Kit stiffen against him, Stephen realized he'd said the wrong thing, and rapidly backpedaled. "Not that it's your—I mean—I didn't—"

Kit pulled free of his arms, her hands on her hips, her eyes flashing gold fire. "And just whose fault is it that we've had such a miserable time?" she demanded.

"Well, you're the one who quit!"

"Oh, right. I was the one who refused to turn around and say something. Give me a break! Just one word, Stephen, and I would have stayed. Not that you wouldn't have forced me out anyway, nine months down the road."

Stephen's lips twitched. "You give me a little too much credit, love. Flattering as it is, I doubt I'd prove to be quite that prolific on the first go." He tilted his head to one side, his brow wrinkled thoughtfully. "Although considering your penchant for accidents..."

Color burned in Kit's cheeks. "Very funny. Did you come all the way up here to exchange insults or did you—did you—"

"Have a change of heart?"

Kit bit down on her lip and turned away from him. *Yes! Yes! Yes!* If the last two weeks had been hell for him, they'd been worse for her. Her emotions were in shreds, her pride, her determination were nonexistent. She'd already decided that she'd do whatever he asked, even knowing what it would entail, what she'd have to give up. Nothing mattered anymore, as long as they were together. But it didn't mean that it wouldn't hurt, and hurt terribly.

"Kit, I love you."

The tears started again. She hadn't a hope of preventing them, nor could she conceal them from Stephen. She heard his soft groan before he pulled her back into his arms, rocking her gently.

"Don't sweetheart. I'm so sorry. I should have tried to explain things before. But I'd never been willing to face the facts till now. I'd never—never realized why I felt the way I did."

"I don't understand," Kit managed to whisper. "You're not making any sense."

He didn't say anything immediately, and when he did it was with obvious reluctance. "My sister." His voice cracked unexpectedly and he cleared his throat, taking a deep breath before continuing. "I told you I had a sister and—and that she died."

Kit nodded, concerned by the harshness of his voice and by the wealth of pain she could hear in the quietly spoken words. What had his sister to do with their situation? And what in the world had happened in his past to cause him this much distress?

Stephen looked down at Kit, cupping her face and tenderly wiping the tears from her cheeks. "Her name was Carrie. And she was sweet and gentle and beautiful. And she drowned when she was five. It was on my eighth birthday."

Kit felt the tears well up again at the stark statement, feeling his agony as though it were her own. "Oh, Stephen." She shook her head, unable to express her sympathy, words sadly inadequate. "What happened?" she asked instead, realizing the story was somehow relevant to their relationship.

Stephen sighed. "I suppose I should actually start from the time my father died."

"In a car accident, wasn't it?"

Stephen nodded. "Mother was pregnant with Carrie. There was no insurance, no money. Dad had a younger brother, Lydia's father, who offered what emotional and financial support he could. But he was very young. Too young to take responsibility for a three-year-old boy and a pregnant woman."

"What did your mother do?" Kit asked, wondering how she would have survived under similar circumstances and prayed fervently that she'd never have to find out. "Did she have any family to turn to?"

"None. She did the only thing she *could* do—she got a job. And worked very, very hard to make ends meet." Stephen shook his head, as though it was beyond his comprehension how his mother had managed. "In those days, women didn't have careers the way they do now." He grimaced at Kit's expression. "I know, I know. Point taken. You can wipe that smug little look off your face."

"So—"

"So, as you are well aware, women weren't paid all that much, certainly not the same as their male counterparts, who were expected to be the main breadwinners. She quickly realized she was going nowhere and had to do something about it."

"That's when she started Clairington?" Kit asked, leaning away from him slightly.

Stephen nodded, tucking her firmly back against him. "It was touch and go for a while there, but as you know, she succeeded beyond belief. The business took off and demanded more and more of her time."

"She must have felt very torn," Kit offered carefully, remembering the one other time she'd attempted to defend his mother, only to have him practically take her head off. "She must have been desperate to make sure you were financially secure. I know those years of struggle would have frightened me pretty badly. Victoria must have been determined never to go back to how it had been."

Stephen's mouth tightened. "So determined that she neglected her children in favor of that damn business."

"A business that supported all of you and kept you together," Kit pointed out tartly.

"A business that consumed all of her, bit by bit, until there was nothing left for her children! Just how much money did she need? Once she'd made enough for us to live comfortably, she should have devoted more time to her family and less to her work." Stephen stopped abruptly, swearing beneath his breath. He glanced down at Kit, ruefully apologetic.

"Sorry, love. Sour grapes. I didn't mean to take it out on you. Believe it or not, I came to terms with those feelings long ago. I do realize that it was very difficult for her and that she did what she thought best at the time. I don't mean to sound so bitter."

"Why shouldn't you be bitter?" Kit answered, understanding how he felt, but not able to agree. "It's because of those feelings that you won't marry a career woman. Stephen, we've been through all this—"

"No, Kit," Stephen interrupted impatiently. "At one time, I admit, I convinced myself that that was the one and only reason for wanting a traditional sort of wife, but it isn't true. Rationally, objectively, I truly believe my mother did what she had to do. I just used those childhood resentments to justify my—my—"

"Prejudice?" Kit offered smoothly.

"My preferences. And don't be flippant. This isn't easy for me, you know."

"And it is for me?" Kit retorted, stung.

"Dammit, Kit! Do you think I'd be here if I didn't care—if I didn't want you enough to tell you these things?" He gripped her arms, pushing her back a step, so that she could see his expression.

His eyes were fixed on her with an intensity that was inescapable. But there was something else Kit could read in that sapphire gaze—an emotion that caused her stomach to tighten and a hot flush to sear her entire body.

"I want you, Kit. I want you so badly that I can't think, I can't eat, I can't sleep. I can't breathe without you there to make the next breath worth taking." Then, in a low, husky voice he added, "I love you, Kit."

"Oh, Stephen."

Kit's arms were around his neck, her fingers deep in Stephen's thick, gold hair, pulling his head downward. And then his lips were on hers, the kiss shattering in its power over her. She couldn't get close enough, couldn't be held tightly enough. She needed him, loved him more than she had thought possible. And she had to tell him, let him know how she felt.

"I love you, Stephen." The words came out in a rush. "I don't care about anything else anymore. It's not worth fighting over. Nothing is more important than how we feel. I'll do whatever you want, but please, please don't leave me."

"No, Kit. No."

"Stephen—" She couldn't keep the desperation from her voice.

"Stop it, Kit!" He gripped her arms and pushed her away from him again, giving her a gentle shake. "I want you to listen to me. I'm not that lonely, resentful child anymore. I grew up. I realized that my mother did the only thing she could in order for us to survive. I freely admit that I wouldn't mind having a traditional sort of wife. But it isn't because of my mother's preoccupation with work that I feel that way. I'm not quite that unreasonable. There's more to it than that."

Kit stared up at him in confusion, struggling to understand what he was trying to tell her. "Then why? Why are you so unwilling to have a working wife?"

"Not a working wife. A working *mother!* Oh, damn." He released her, rubbing his face in weary resignation, forcing himself to continue his story. "Once Clairington took off, Mother was able to buy a real home for us. A huge, gorgeous place with what seemed like a thousand rooms. There was a housekeeper, a nanny, a yard that went on forever, and the ultimate luxury—a swimming pool."

He was speaking faster now. "She promised she'd be home. She'd gone in to work to finish just a few more things and then we were going to celebrate my birthday. It was going to be a swimming party. But it got later and later and she never came. If only she had come!" There was an urgent pleading in his voice, like a child's begging to be woken from a terrifying nightmare. "If only she'd been there, Carrie never would have gotten so tired of waiting. She wouldn't have decided to go in. Carrie—Carrie—"

He couldn't finish, but he didn't need to. It was obvious what had happened. His little sister had drowned. The waiting had become too much, the pool too great a temptation for a little girl promised a swimming party.

Kit slid her arms around Stephen, hugging him, trying to fill his stiff, cold body with all the warmth and comfort she had to offer. "Don't, Stephen! Don't torture your-self. None of you could have known that would happen."

"I blamed my mother." His words were muffled against her hair. "I said horrible things to her, unforgivable things."

"You were only eight, Stephen," Kit argued gently. "Victoria doesn't give the impression of a woman holding a grudge. In fact, she acts more like a mother wanting to reestablish a relationship with her son."

He turned sad, regretful blue eyes on her. "I swore to her that I'd never marry a businesswoman, that my wife would look after our children. She'd keep them safe and never neglect them and they'd never feel lonely or be killed." He bowed his head. "I screamed those words at her that day."

Kit stroked his arm, searching for the words that would console him. "Stephen, you were a child. A child who hit out. A child who probably felt every bit as guilty as his mother." She felt the muscles of his arm tense beneath her fingers and knew she'd hit a nerve.

"You did feel guilty, didn't you?" Kit breathed, under-standing finally dawning. *Oh, Stephen,* she thought, *what a terrible thing to live with all these years.* How did you manage to deal with those self-punishing feelings for so long? To never speak of it, to always carry it around with you, must have been hell on earth. "You couldn't be expected to handle the guilt, my love. It's only natural that you'd try to dump it on the one person who felt just as re-sponsible as you did. And undoubtedly she accepted the blame and added her own to it.

"But it wasn't your fault Carrie died, Stephen," Kit continued urgently. "You can't watch a child every sec-ond. Your mother could have been home and it still might have happened. What about the nanny and the house-   ner? They were there, weren't they?" He nodded, and   he implication sink in. "And Carrie still died." She shook her head, striving for a lighter tone. "It's no wonder you're so protective of Lydia. I'm surprised you didn't kill me when she fainted that day."

An answering smile briefly touched his mouth. "Believe it or not, I'm even more protective of you. Why do you think I'm so nervous about those lab experiments of yours? My heart is permanently lodged in my mouth when you're in one of your creative moods."

Kit let that one pass. "Carrie's death was a tragic accident," she stated firmly. "But it wasn't any one person's fault."

"I know. I know that now. It's been a long time coming, but I think I've finally come to terms with it. I guess I've realized it's time to let my mother off the hook—and myself." His voice was weary, but accepting. "I talked to her about Carrie's death, laid it all out and told her how I've felt all these years."

"Your mother was willing to talk about Carrie?"

Stephen nodded. "It was the first time we'd ever mentioned what happened since that day, let alone discussed her death openly and frankly. And you're right. I blamed myself every bit as much as I blamed Mother. I'd just never been able to face it before."

"What did Victoria say?"

He was silent, remembering. "She cried," he finally answered. "I held her in my arms and she cried till there were no tears left. I think it helped heal us both—cauterized the wound, I guess."

"And now?" she dared to ask.

Stephen met her eyes directly. "I was wrong, Kit. That's what I came to tell you. I was wrong to believe that a traditional wife was any sort of guarantee that life would be safe. I think, subconsciously, that's why I wanted the woman I married to be home with the children. To protect them from harm. But you're right. Parents can't watch their children every second. It could just as easily have happened while my mother was there. You read about it all the time.''

"And now?'' she repeated, more anxiously.

Unexpectedly he began to chuckle, relaxing, his somber expression completely gone. "Well, my little jinx, I can definitely say that marriage to you won't give me any guarantees of safety.''

Kit made a face at him. "Cute. But it doesn't answer my question. Where does that leave us?''

He captured a strand of her hair, running it between his fingers. "Married, if you'll have me.''

"If I'll—'' Kit took a deep breath. "What do you think, you impossible man? You think I've been moping around the last fourteen days for the fun of it? Of course I'll marry you!''

"Good.'' He rubbed his hands together briskly. "Things are a mess at work. Todd can't do a damn thing with that tarantula of yours. The producers are screaming blue murder. And there's some hitch with the squirt guns that needs to be worked out, but I'm sure it isn't anything you can't handle....'' He stopped, grinning down at her. "You did want to come back to work, didn't you?''

Did she want...? Kit tried to decide which method of murder she should use on him. But she never had a chance to choose, Stephen's kiss driving every thought from her head save one. She yanked herself free of his embrace. "And are the problems at work the only reason you want me back, or—''

She never finished the sentence, his second, longer kiss the best response he could give her.

"Does that answer your question?''

Kit nodded happily, until she remembered the one subject they'd assiduously avoided. "Stephen, we haven't discussed—''

"I know." She could see the tension returning to his face. He ran a hand nervously through his hair. "Kids, right?"

"Kids," Kit agreed.

"I'll do my best, Kit. That's all I can say. But I can't promise I won't worry—" He searched her face a trifle anxiously. "I know it's wrong to ask, but tell me you'll put the children first, that you won't—"

Kit shook her head. "No, Stephen," she told him tenderly, firmly. "You will always come first with me, and *then* our children. But I'll love them more than I can possibly express, and I'll always put our family ahead of my job." She looked into his eyes, adding softly, "And I'll do my very, very best to keep them safe and protected. Do you really think I could do anything else, feel any other way?"

Stephen swallowed tightly. "I love you so much, Kit." He glanced over his shoulder toward the house. "I guess we should get back and let your parents know how things stand."

"There's plenty of time." A slow, sensuous smile spread across Kit's face. "I can think of one or two things I'd rather do first."

From the house, a grinning Christopher and Elizabeth watched as two figures merged into one.

CHAPTER ELEVEN

"SHH, VIKI'S ASLEEP," Kit warned as Stephen wearily entered their bedroom and collapsed on top of the mattress. "Have the police and fire trucks finally gone? Did you explain that it was just an accident?"

"I did. Although I think they've come to view our little 'accidents' with a rather jaundiced eye." Stephen yawned widely. "You were right about the captain having a little one at home—I just can't quite figure out how you knew. I showed him our new line of baby toys, as you suggested, and it seems to have done the trick. He did...suggest... that we strongly discourage Todd from any further impromptu firework displays."

Kit smothered a grin. "Todd appeared suitably chastised when I last saw him. He just wanted to give Viki something special for her first birthday, and since she was a Fourth-of-July baby, he thought..."

"I know what our dear Mr. Templeton thought," Stephen stated grimly. "And the next time I see him, he's going to learn what I—"

"I was amazed that Viki enjoyed it so much," Kit interrupted hastily, making a mental note to warn Todd to keep a low profile for the next few days. "I was sure all the noise and excitement would frighten her."

Stephen snorted. "You must be joking—your daughter letting a few explosions and bright lights scare her? She was in her element!"

"Beast!" Kit sank onto the bed, snuggling up against him. "Have I told you recently how much I love you?"

Stephen wrapped his arms around her, pulling her firmly up against him. "It's been at least an hour. Tell me again." And he kissed her thoroughly when she'd happily complied. "It's all worked out well, hasn't it, my little jinx? The last twenty months, I mean."

"Twenty-one months. Remember?" Kit corrected, a tiny smile curling her mouth. "Viki was born nine months to the day after our wedding."

Stephen chuckled. "How could I forget? You teased me unmercifully about that."

Kit laughed, too, thinking about how they'd worried so unnecessarily the first year of their marriage. The compromises they'd made had been surprisingly minor, and the love and joy they'd experienced as a result, amazingly intense. "And yes, everything has worked out well. Your mother's idea for starting up a day-care center on the premises was brilliant. I wish I could take the credit for that little gem."

"Well, you were the one to suggest Miss Dobson as the head of the project. And she does seem to enjoy it much more than the retirement she'd initially suggested."

Kit giggled. "She's perfect at it—she only misplaced Viki that one time! And we did find her safe and sound in the broom closet, playing with those baby Tarantula Terrors."

Stephen glared indignantly down at her. "At least Miss Dobson doesn't subject *my* daughter to mad experiments in that lab of yours."

"Oh-ho. If it hadn't been for my experimenting with *your* daughter, *your* bank account wouldn't be quite so healthy. Those ideas we've come up with for newborns were all thanks to Viki. Besides—" her eyes twinkled teasingly up at him "—it was the only legitimate excuse I could think of for bringing her to work with me. After all,

I had to try out my ideas with a live baby. And Viki did fit the bill.''

Stephen rolled over on top of her, crushing her beneath him in a very satisfactory manner. "You're lucky Mother allows it. She takes her role as grandmama very seriously. Do you think it's because Viki's her namesake?"

Kit shook her head firmly, winding her arms around his neck. "I think your mother is reveling in diapers and nursery rhymes and trips to the park. Fortunately, Lydia's due next month and then Victoria can start indulging herself with her newest grandchild. I get the feeling she's making up for all the things she missed doing when you were a baby." Serious gold eyes met sapphire ones. "Does it still hurt, Stephen? Seeing your mother give Viki all that she neglected to give you?"

A gentle smile spread across Stephen's face. "No," he stated positively. "It's such a relief to see her so happy and carefree that I'm willing to give her half a dozen grandchildren if it means she'll always be that way."

"Six?" Kit choked.

"Well, maybe you and Lydia could come to some sort of arrangement about dividing them up between— Hey!" he complained as a pillow landed on his head.

"You deserved it," Kit informed him tartly, then peeped up at him from beneath her lashes, a strange gleam sparkling in her eyes. "And you should watch what you wish for—you *did* know that twins run in my family, didn't you?"

"Twins?" Stephen repeated a trifle faintly, frowning down at her. "You mean, two—like Viki?" He remembered with a sinking feeling the mischief his just barely walking infant seemed to generate with as much frequency as her mother.

"Like Viki, only worse," Kit hastened to inform him, tongue firmly in cheek. "Don't forget—there's twice the fertile imagination to draw on." She let that sink in before murmuring, "It's late, Stephen. Why don't you get out of those sooty clothes and then we can—" She breathed a soft suggestion in his ear.

"Sure, sounds great. Uh, you were just kidding about twins, weren't you, Kit? *Kit?*"

But Kit only smiled a funny little smile, and tugged her husband's head down toward hers. "Why don't we start working on it right away and see?" she suggested huskily. Maybe tomorrow she'd let him off the hook. Then again, maybe she'd tell him about the two sets of triplets on her mother's side. . . .

Six exciting series for you every month... from Harlequin

Harlequin Romance
The series that started it all

Tender, captivating and heartwarming...
love stories that sweep you off to faraway places
and delight you with the magic of love.

◆

Harlequin Presents
Powerful contemporary love stories...as individual as the women who read them

The No. 1 romance series...
exciting love stories for you, the woman of today...
a rare blend of passion and dramatic realism.

◆

Harlequin Superromance®
It's more than romance... it's Harlequin Superromance

A sophisticated, contemporary romance-fiction
series, providing you with a longer,
more involving read...a richer mix of complex plots,
realism and adventure.

Harlequin
American Romance™
Harlequin celebrates the American woman...

...by offering you romance stories written about American women, by American women for American women. This series offers you contemporary romances uniquely North American in flavor and appeal.

◆

Harlequin Temptation™
Passionate stories for today's woman

An exciting series of sensual, mature stories of love...dilemmas, choices, resolutions... all contemporary issues dealt with in a true-to-life fashion by some of your favorite authors.

◆

Harlequin Intrigue™
Because romance can be quite an adventure

Harlequin Intrigue, an innovative series that blends the romance you expect... with the unexpected. Each story has an added element of intrigue that provides a new twist to the Harlequin tradition of romance excellence.

Harlequin Books

PROD-A-2

You'll flip . . . your pages won't!
Read paperbacks *hands-free* with

Book Mate · I

The perfect "mate" for all your romance paperbacks

**Traveling • Vacationing • At Work • In Bed • Studying
• Cooking • Eating**

Perfect size for all standard paperbacks, this wonderful invention makes reading a pure pleasure! Ingenious design holds paperback books OPEN and FLAT so even wind can't ruffle pages – leaves your hands free to do other things. Reinforced, wipe-clean vinyl-covered holder flexes to let you turn pages without undoing the strap . . . supports paperbacks so well, they have the strength of hardcovers!

Pages turn WITHOUT opening the strap

SEE-THROUGH STRAP

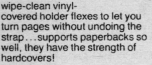

Reinforced back stays flat

Built in bookmark

BOOK MARK

BACK COVER HOLDING STRIP

10 x 7¼ opened
Snaps closed for easy carrying, too